D

OR

DEFEND

A DELIGHTFULLY DEADLY
NOVEL

BY GAIL CARRIGER

The Finishing School
Etiquette & Espionage
Curtsies & Conspiracies
Waistcoats & Weaponry
Manners & Mutiny

Delightfully Deadly Novellas
Poison or Protect
Defy or Defend

The Parasol Protectorate
Soulless
Changeless
Blameless
Heartless
Timeless

Supernatural Society Novellas
Romancing the Inventor
Romancing the Werewolf

The Custard Protocol
Prudence
Imprudence
Competence
Reticence

Claw & Courtship Novellas
How to Marry a Werewolf

AS G. L. CARRIGER

Marine Biology (prequel short story free
With Gail's newsletter: The Chirrup)
The Sumage Solution
The Omega Objection
The Enforcer Enigma

The Tinkered Stars
The 5th Gender

DEFY
OR
DEFEND

A DELIGHTFULLY DEADLY
NOVEL

GAIL CARRIGER

GAIL CARRIGER LLC

GAIL CARRIGER, LLC

gailcarriger.com

ACKNOWLEDGEMENTS

Thank you so much to my wonderful team. My patient beta readers (Rachel, Marie, Amber, Tanya, and Chanie, who did this over the holidays!), my awesome developmental editor Sue Brown-Moore (who terrified me with many pages of edits but it turned out to be all okay), my lovely copy editors Shelley Bates and Flo Selfman (both of whom make time for me and tell me they love my work, even though they really don't have to), and my formatter Nina Pierce.

CHAPTER ONE

In Which There May, or May Not, Be Sparkles

March 1869
(Just prior to the introduction of the bustle. No, really, it's important to know this.)

Sir Crispin Bontwee chivvied up to an impressively large chartreuse front door with a sense of overwhelming relief. Not because of the color of the door, mind you (which was a touch assertive, frankly, for a door – what did it think it was playing at?) but because of the possibilities that lay behind it.

The door opened, and the possibilities proved themselves to be a female of biblical proportions and eccentric dress. She was that particular style of solid British womanhood that held firm against both military invasion and recalcitrant pie crusts, rolling pin wielded with consummate skill in either case.

Sir Crispin knew her of old.

He bowed slightly and hid his grin, because both woman and door demanded respect. "My dear Madame, what a pleasure to see you again."

"It's you, is it?" Mrs Bagley pursed her lips to hide her delight and threw the door wide.

"At your service." He strode inside, fairly vibrating with suppressed excitement. It had been ages since his last mission. He was restless with a need to fix something, or rescue someone, or perhaps both.

Today Mrs Bagley was dressed like a butler. She looked rather dashing, truth be told. Her cravat was chartreuse to match the door and her striped waistcoat was cut to perfection. Cris was mildly perturbed by the fact that trousers suited her demeanor better than they did most men of his acquaintance. It could have been worse – Mrs Bagley had once answered the door dressed as a yellow butterfly. Or was it a moth? Regardless, a winged cape had been involved. One was never certain what *exactly* Bertie's housekeeper would be wearing on any given evening. It was one of the most exciting things about Bertie's household.

"I've been *summoned*, Madame." Cris always referred to Mrs Bagley as *Madame*. *Mrs Bagley* suited her ill, and anything more informal from Cris would cause a one-woman riot. Mrs Bagley took meticulous handling. He didn't envy Bertie.

Mrs Bagley widened her eyes at him in pretend shock. "*Summoned*, were you indeed? Wipe your feet, young man."

Cris was already wiping them. Mrs Bagley's favorite thing was to give orders she knew were already being obeyed. She didn't even pause for breath. "A new mission, is it?"

"Now, Madame, I can't discuss such things with you, even if I had an inkling." Cris drew himself up, but only a little – wouldn't do to loom over a woman like Mrs Bagley.

"As you're very well aware, I'll hear about it later."

"Of course you will, although I'm not supposed to know that. I must say, it's a good thing you're on our side." He twitched towards the hallway, needing to move past niceties into useful activity.

"Are you sure about that?" She pretended a wicked glare.

"I live in fear, dear Madame. We all do. No doubt the fate of the War Office rests upon your discretion. Now, where is he?"

"In the conservatory, of course. Is he ever anywhere else?" Mrs Bagley marched off. Cris strode eagerly after, careful not to overtake her. It was pleasing to trail behind a woman who walked like she had places to be and people to kill.

The hallway was scrupulously clean and well maintained, despite the fact that the walls were lined with hundreds of tiny drawers topped by glass-fronted curio cases. There might, just possibly, have been wallpaper behind it all, but no one would ever know.

Bertie was a dedicated dilettante who picked up and put down interests obsessively. They walked past a beautifully mounted collection of wooden ladles (not *spoons*, *ladles*) and a display of Bertie's own taxidermic caterpillars. It was a little like the natural history museum, only more eclectic, and with no apparent curation or connection between one case and the next.

Cris was so accustomed to the spectacle he barely

glanced at the curiosities.

Mrs Bagley paused mid-hallway (much to his frustration) and turned on Cris, contorting her face into one of concern. It didn't work well, as she was not a particularly sympathetic person, so her face went a little twitchy with the effort.

"Most distressing to hear about your father, Sir Crispin. I am sorry for your loss."

What Cris wanted to say was, *Hang my father, everyone I know is delighted that he's dead*, but one didn't do that to a housekeeper, especially not Mrs Bagley. Plus, as an Englishman, Crispin didn't like making others uncomfortable with real feelings.

So he drew his own face into an expression of sorrow and said politely, "Thank you kindly, Madame."

Niceties observed, the housekeeper marched on, eventually opening the double doors to the conservatory with a jerk. Then, because it would take too long to find him amongst all the plants, she raised her voice in the manner of a governess, and yelled into the teeming verdancy, "Bertie, you blighter! Sir Crispin is here to see you."

Bertie was undergoing a cactus stage. Had been for near on a year now. It was getting increasingly prickly at his house, particularly in the conservatory.

Accordingly, Bertie appeared from behind a large, fluffy bit of shrubbery clutching a pot from which protruded a small round cactus with a single bright pink flower. It so closely resembled a hedgehog wearing a hat that Cris was mildly startled not to see it sprout little legs and waddle off.

"Crispy, my *dear* fellow! What a lovely surprise to see you."

"*You* summoned *me*, Bertie." Cris spread his hands wide in supplication.

"Did I? How very peculiar of me. Have you met an *Echinocereus engelmannii* before? Isn't it remarkable? This one just flowered. I think it's rather jolly, don't you?"

"Looks like a hedgehog in a hat." Cris was one for honesty when it didn't matter or hurt anyone's feelings. He then took off his own hat and looked for a place to put it. There wasn't one. So he put it back on his head. He'd never dare give it to Mrs Bagley.

"Fantastic, I say. I shall name it Wobesmere. Note the shortness of the internode? Just there? No, don't touch! Nasty things, cacti. Now, let me tell you, one of the most remarkable things about them is the areoles. You see this bit here—"

Mrs Bagley interrupted him, crimson-faced. "*Really*, Bertie, Sir Crispin is suffering a great loss at the moment. Do stop prattling on at the poor fellow."

"Really? What's he lost?" Bertie had a large straight nose, beady dark eyes, and a wide smiling mouth. He had unfortunately fine hair, close cut, that had gone gray when they were at university together and begun a brave retreat some years later, so that he now resembled a surprised but cuddly mongoose. He mostly acted like one too, chattering and familiar, unless a snake was about. Then he proved quite deadly.

"His father, you nubbin." Mrs Bagley indicated Crispin's mourning attire with a flick of two fingers.

Cris would have preferred Bertie continue on in ignorance and get to the mission, but Mrs Bagley was clearly having none of that.

Bertie, a true friend, instantly forgot about the cactus and its areoles and dashed forward to clutch one of Crispin's hands in his own, waving the cactus about dangerously with the other. "My dear Crispy, forgive me. I entirely forgot. Do come in. Sit down, sit down. Oh, there isn't anywhere to sit, is there? Wait a moment. Eudora, would you be a dove and move those whatever-they-ares off that bench-seat-thingame there? Yes, I know, this is business. We ought to go to the study, but I don't feel right leaving the *engelmannii* alone right now, not when it's in the midst of flowering for the first time. Might put it off. You understand, don't you, Eudora? No, you don't, do you. Well, Crispy understands, don't you, old chap? There, see? Sit down, do."

Cris sat, minding his posture and trying desperately to sit still, while Mrs Bagley scowled affectionately and made room for them both.

Bertie plonked down next to Cris, cactus on his lap.

"Crispy, my dear fellow, you do look peaky. You must be terribly worn down. The funeral was ghastly, I suspect?"

"Utterly. All of my sisters were there. *All of them.*" Cris shuddered to recall his trying morning. "They enjoyed themselves tremendously, of course. Wept a great deal, even wailed once in a while. London now has a decided surfeit of damp handkerchiefs." He'd not seen the like since his brother's funeral, when they'd all been much younger, with more excuses for pejorative histrionics. One might hope sisters would have grown out of such things. Or at least cry less for a lesser man. Apparently not.

Bertie looked imploringly at his housekeeper. "Might we have tea, please, Eudora my dove? I ask not for me, of course, but for my dear bereaved friend."

Mrs Bagley rolled her eyes and left the conservatory without comment.

Bertie turned back to Cris. "Are the sisters still trying to marry you off?"

"Desperately. They even brought prospects to the funeral." Cris rolled his shoulders back and assumed a falsetto voice. "Oh Crispin, darling, have you met my husband's second cousin Patricia? She's doing very interesting things with cross-stitching these days. Or Eugenia – have you met Eugenia? Eugenia collects pen nibs, I'll have you know."

Bertie grimaced. "You poor fellow. It's one of my great joys in life that I was never saddled with sisters."

"Count those blessings, Bertie, do."

Bertie's expression turned suddenly serious. Certainly more serious than a funeral warranted. "You don't owe the world for what he was, old fellow. You know that, don't you? You can't fix the sins of your father. None of us can. 'Specially when the bounder's dead."

But Crispin *did* owe the world and he *would* try. Because his father had been a rat bastard, squeezing and taking and abusing, and Crispin had built his whole life around being something that wasn't that. It was part of the reason he worked for the War Office.

He fiddled with a sherd of flowerpot. "Best thing the blighter's ever done, die. Now, if we might get on? What exactly am I doing here? Not that I don't enjoy a visit. But even you can't have simply invited me 'round to show off your latest prickly acquisition. Well, I mean you can have, but even you rarely stoop so low on the day of a family funeral. Please tell me you have some useful employment for me? How may I serve my country today?"

"Actually, I do have something for you, Crispy." There was a set to Bertie's eyebrows that suggested Cris wasn't going to like the next bit. He wracked his brain to think who might be back from a mission and ready to go out into the fray again.

"Oh no. Not Sparkles." He pointed the bit of broken flowerpot at Bertie, accusingly.

Bertie coughed. "I'm afraid so, old chap. We've activated the Honey Bee Initiative."

"Oh no, Bertie, please say you didn't. Not after I just spent all day with my sisters." Cris hopped up and started pacing. The Honey Bee called for pacing.

"She's really very good. I don't know why she frustrates you so."

"You wouldn't. You get along with everyone. That's why you're so good at your job. But honestly, she's so much work for whoever is assigned to be safety. She's always wandering off."

"That's your complaint?"

Cris thumped back on the bench and slouched, tilting his head to look up and out the vaulted glass ceiling of Bertie's conservatory. He intended this to show Bertie the depths of his frustration. He could see the occasional dirigible bobbing by. He knew there were stars beyond, but London was so bright at night in these times of ready gaslight, it was near impossible to see them. Cris missed the stars.

Honey Bee. Of course it would be.

She was one of the best the War Office had on retainer, for the gentler jobs. Trained at the greatest Finishing School ever to float. Exactly the right combination of pretty, charming, and evasive. (Although not particularly bloodthirsty, thank heavens. He got the impression that the Honey Bee didn't enjoy actually hurting people. This was regarded as a minor failing by the uppity-ups, which is why they so often paired her with a soldier like Cris. Soldiers could kill if necessary.)

Sir Crispin found her sweet enough to be difficult, chattery enough to be annoying, and jolly enough to affect even his unflappable demeanor. Even knowing she was capable, Cris worried about her constantly when they were on a mission together. This was, of course, one of her skills – convincing others that she needed looking after.

Silence had stretched while Bertie stared at him.

"There is also her hair to consider." Cris tried to defend his position. He'd lost sleep over that hair.

"Her hair? What on earth's wrong with it?"

Cris shrugged, realizing he'd made a gaffe. "There's a lot of it, that's all." It was sort of buttery and curly and a little wild. He wanted to run his fingers through it, press his cheek into it. He was going to add something about her skin too, which was creamy and probably petal soft, but that would surely put him in danger of discovery. The Honey Bee was prone to driving his fancies into places only his bounder of a father would understand. Cris didn't want to take advantage of Sparkles, never that.

Except that of course he did want, wanted so very much to corrupt her in the worst way, and therein lay a massive, creamy-skinned, honey-haired mess of a problem.

Bertie was looking at him oddly, but fortunately, Mrs Bagley came in carrying a generous tea tray, which she set down with a clatter.

Cris stood to help her settle it – it looked a bit heavy.

Bertie's expression was all excitement. "Are those roly-poly puddings? Delightful! Thank you, Eudora."

Mrs Bagley glared at her employer. "You aren't abusing poor Sir Crispin, are you, Mr Luckinbill?"

"Only in the line of duty."

"No more roly-poly for you then. Savor these, for they will be your last." At which she whirled and departed.

Bertie looked after her with soft eyes. "Hard-hearted female."

"Nice to know she's on my side," said Cris, shifting forwards and trying to show a little enthusiasm for the kindness in the offer of tea, if not for the tea itself.

"Women usually are." Bertie gave him the same look he'd been giving him since Eton.

"All except Sparkles," replied Cris. Because she was remarkably resistant to his charms.

"All except her." Bertie, clearly pleased about this,

poured them both tea, adding sugar to his and milk to Crispin's without having to ask. "Why is that, do you feel?"

Cris took the teacup, but set it down without drinking any. He was already sloshing from a day spent commiserating with the bereaved – no need to exacerbate the situation. "She took me in instant dislike, apparently. And she reminds me of my sisters. It allows us to eschew any formality of manner, not to mention prospective affection."

Bertie nibbled his roly-poly pud. "Well, you carry on as her safety however you see fit. It would be better if you two had a decent working relationship, however, for queen and country and all that rot."

"I'll do my best to behave."

"It's not your behavior I worry about, old chap. Never is."

"So you see what I mean? She's difficult, prone to trouble."

Bertie looked noncommittal. "Mmm. Speaking of – your mission."

"Speak on, do. I'm at your disposal."

"It's not mine you have to be at, it's BUR's."

Crispin's leg began to jiggle at that. "Crickets, what's the bureau want with me and the Honey Bee, for goodness' sake? We're both well out of their purview. Quite apart from everything else, we're human. We handle human problems. Not the supernatural." He suppressed a shudder.

Bertie grimaced. "That's the thing, they decided they needed daylight players for this one. They *have* humans on retainer, of course they do, but none trained in quite the same manner as our Honey Bee. BUR's tactics are more... last resort. Violent and final, if you follow my meaning."

"The Honey Bee is good at fixing things. BUR is better at ending them." Cris nodded and tried not to worry.

"Exactly so." Bertie made a face, as though he'd smelled something unpleasant. "Lord Maccon leans in favor of direct and fatal. You know werewolves. Such can be useful, but this particular infiltration requires subtlety."

"And your first thought was, of course, *Sparkles*?"

"Don't be mean, Crispy. She can be subtle, in the right way. In the necessary way and when the situation demands it. You've seen her work. She's good."

Cris sighed, defeated. "Very good, actually. Go on." She was flirtatious and conniving and heart-stopping. He adored her, of course.

"The Bureau of Unnatural Registry has recently had word of trouble at a vampire hive up in Nottingham. It seems to be going a touch *off* – not to put too fine a point on it. The queen has come over loopy, holed herself up in a limestone cave or some such nonsense, communicating solely by means of homemade Valentine's cards."

Cris frowned. Not that he was sentimental, but— "It's April, Bertie."

"Precisely! And I mean to say, the kind of cards with gold and lace and bits of ribbon stuck to them. She seems to have been doing this for months, if not years. There's not a confident timeline. BUR only recently noticed. At last report, a decade ago, it was a small, staid, stable hive – nothing to fret about. Now limestone caves and Valentine's cards out of season. You see the source of the distress? The rest of her hive is unresponsive to BUR's inquiries as to why she's retreated. But they are essentially without a queen. However, as they've done nothing supernaturally *wrong*, the Bureau's agents are stymied. No apparent crimes against humanity either, no rash of murders or disappearances in the area, so they can't send in the constabulary to get all constabby-stabby. They have lost most of their drones to abandonment, not death. So there's a chance the vampires are starving themselves out of pure stubbornness. It's all rather a mess. Wants sorting. BUR came to us and I'm sending in the Honey Bee. You know how she gets when things want tidying. You're to go along to keep everything under control."

"You want to fix a vampire hive using *Sparkles*?"

"That's the general idea. Usually works. Vampires like shiny things. The Honey Bee is awfully shiny."

Cris pressed his hand to his own leg to stop its vibrating, not liking the idea of Dimity Plumleigh-Teignmott loose in some bally vampire hive. "I've read her file. I thought she fainted at the sight of blood."

Bertie waved his hand. "Only very large amounts and under particularly stressful circumstances. Minor impediment. I'm sure you'll manage to control for triggering variables."

"It's a *vampire* hive, Bertie, you wiffin."

"You'll be all right."

"I hate it when you say that." Sir Crispin gave up

trying to be still, stood, and began to wander about. Not quite pacing, but nearly there.

"Yes, but see how distracted you are now? All your dead-father troubles forgotten."

"To be supplanted with *sparkling* new troubles."

"Exactly. Speaking of, where is he?"

"Where's who?" Cris whirled to look at the closed conservatory door.

"*He* would be late. I asked a friend 'round, in case you had vampire-related questions. This not being your field of study, nor mine either, quite frankly, and BUR being mostly run by werewolves these days, I thought we might consult with an outside expert."

The double doors to the conservatory burst open in a dramatic way, displaying an enthusiasm they'd not shown when Cris walked through. An impossibly glorious person swept into the room, his steps small and his arm gestures prodigious.

It was harder than one might think, to flirt a gentleman inventor into submission. Any given inventor might be susceptible, but was usually so confused at getting feminine attention it took extra effort (on the part of said femininity) to get the blighter up and running.

Miss Dimity Plumleigh-Teignmott would never admit she was struggling with this particular inventor. Yet... she struggled.

Honestly, sometimes setting a lady of Dimity's caliber at an inventor was unfair to all parties concerned.

This particular inventor, one Professor Meeld-Forrison, had responded to Dimity's initial foray with the rapidity of an allergic reaction, and had retreated into almost complete silence at the merest hint of a fluttered eyelash. When she fiddled with the massive sapphire brooch at her collar (to draw attention to the whiteness of her throat, of course), he nearly fainted.

Have you any idea how hard it is to flirt with someone who won't even talk back, let alone flirt back?

They had not covered this particular level of resistance at Finishing School.

Dimity had been at the endeavor for over half an hour with little conversation, let alone results. She'd exhausted all possible topics of discourse, from books to vehicles to steam technology, from hounds to whiskey to all manner of things that interested any given gentleman, intellectual or otherwise. The man seemed to be composed entirely of monosyllabic murmurs of mild-mannered agreement.

She might recommend blowing up Big Ben and replacing it with a spun sugar poodle and Professor Meeld-Forrison would merely say, "Mum-hum."

Which, to be fair, made him excellent husband material, but the worst source for information during an espionage operation.

But Dimity was resilient. Dimity was determined. Dimity could handle anything.

Except shy.

And this poor fellow seemed almost paralytically shy.

Dimity nevertheless continued to steer him around his own laboratory and chatter at him. She picked up things, touching them ostentatiously, hoping for some kind of reaction, even anger as he leapt to defend some precious piece of technology from the bumbling female wafting about his domain.

Nothing.

Desperately, Dimity mentioned badminton.

I mean to say, who doesn't have opinions on badminton? *Everyone* has opinions on badminton. The latest dirigible-on-dirigible World Puff had been an absolute *triumph*.

Nothing.

Nothing on badminton from the great Professor Meeld-Forrison. Not the tiniest little puff of interest.

Really, Dimity was beginning to question whether the man was capable of speaking in full sentences, let alone the conversation required in order to sell his technology to the Prussians.

How could any man conduct illegal business with overseas agents when he could barely open his mouth? The War Office must be wrong on this one. This was a waste of her time.

Dimity was well aware that she was an acquired taste – but fortunately, once convinced to try, most people acquired a taste for her rather quickly. She was easy to talk to, for goodness' sake. Easy!

Not so far as Professor Meeld-Forrison was concerned.

Perhaps it wasn't verbal language she need use?

In the guise of delicate avoidance of steam emanating from the corner of the lab, Dimity whipped out her fan. She fluttered at the steam ineffectually, and then shadowed her nose and lower face, tilting her chin down and widening her eyes so they were as big and as limpid as possible.

"Oh, my dear sir, such risks you take for your studies. So many devices all running at once. Surely there is no small danger to your person?"

Words not working, Dimity would try bodies. She sidled closer to the man. Increased her breathing a little. Tried to match hers to his, which had caught and was now quite rapid.

She gazed into his face adoringly. "Dear sir, you must be so strong to have to handle such things, feeding in coal and carrying water and so forth."

Professor Meeld-Forrison cleared his throat and looked like he wanted to flee or faint. Instead, he froze.

The man is completely hopeless, thought Dimity. She angled her body towards him, shifted the shawl away from her white neck, exposing the little divot at the base of her throat.

Still nothing.

Her eyelashes fluttered.

The man swallowed. A tiny bead of sweat appeared at his brow.

Aha! "Dear Professor Meeld-Forrison, you don't speak any other languages, do you? I do so adore a polyglot."

"I speak a little French," he admitted, in a whisper.

"No German?"

"Not a single bratwurst of it, I'm afraid."

Dimity giggled. She wasn't sure he'd meant to be funny, but at least she'd gotten an entire sentence out of the man.

"Oh, are we talking about sausages? I do love a sausage. Are you a sausage or a bacon connoisseur, as a rule, dear Professor?"

The professor's eyes widened. "Uh, bacon, I assure you."

So he liked women in his bed, did he? *At least that's cleared up. Unless he means actual bacon.* But the man was only shy, she suspected, not obtuse.

Dimity moved in for the kill. She took his arm.

He did not flinch this time.

She closed her fan, for it was no longer necessary. He was now looking down into her face, his eyes a little dazed.

She leaned subtly against him, as if dying for his manly arms. His support. His attention.

He shuddered and angled his upper body towards her. He sported the kind of frame that had spent too much time indoors examining devices – curled at the shoulders and bent in the spine.

The bacon has it, thought Dimity.

"Shall we continue our tour, my *dear* sir?" She gave him a slow blink. (Too soon for another eyelash flutter.)

He wobbled slightly and finally came up to bat. "My dear Miss Chitty—"

"Call me Jonquil, do."

"My dear Miss Jonquil, I should like nothing better." His eyes were now fixed on hers, his breathing a little shallow. She hoped he wouldn't faint.

"And shall we talk more about breakfast? Are you a particular fan of the meal?"

"I should like nothing more for the rest of my days," he said, apparently realizing that she was, in fact, flirting with him. Poor chap, he wasn't used to such things.

He patted her hand where she clutched his arm, then very daringly left his cold, clammy one atop hers.

Oh dear, thought Dimity, *I might have taken this a little far.*

"Breakfast first, my dear sir. Now, tell me, have you traveled much? How do you feel about breakfast as served on the Continent? I've been given to understand, for example, that the French prefer a bit of puffy bread and some coffee to start their day. Surely not. Surely that is wicked hearsay."

"Oh no, my dear Miss Jonquil, I understand that's entirely true." The gentleman shook his head. His hair was rather messy, sticking up about a pair of yellow-tinted goggles pushed back from his brow. He looked tired, and older than the mission launch papers had stated.

"You understand? You've never visited yourself?"

"Sadly, no." His eyelashes and eyebrows were so pale they disappeared into his face, making him seem perennially surprised.

"And other parts of Europe?" Dimity pressed, but he shook his head. She had to face the truth – this man wasn't guilty. He hadn't done it. Or if he had passed along illegal technology to the Prussians, he hadn't realized what he'd done.

"Oh, my dear sir, I too am woefully under-traveled. It's nothing to be ashamed of, I assure you. I've barely even met anyone from outside the British Isles. A tragedy of my innocence, I suspect." *Now* was the time for more eyelash fluttering.

Dimity fluttered.

The man melted right there in the middle of his lab. Metaphorically, of course. No actual melting was involved.

Which made Dimity think fondly of sugar melting into tea. She wondered if she could extract Professor Meeld-Forrison to a tea house. She was famished and this was taking longer than she'd anticipated. "Certainly you're more worldly than I, Professor."

The professor cleared his throat and admitted to having met, only recently, at his gentleman's club, several visitors all the way from Prussia.

And that, as they say, was that.

Dimity did not get him out to tea, but she did get the details of most of the conversation with those Prussians. She learned that the gentlemen in question had visited Professor Meeld-Forrison's lab. Flattered by their interest in his work, he had given them an extensive tour, much as he was doing with her now. And so, the whole sordid story played out.

The poor chap hadn't meant to be a traitor. His interests lay entirely in the arena of vacuum technology, what the War Office referred to as *fluff and blow*. There were projectile military applications, but Professor Meeld-Forrison obviously neither knew nor cared.

In Dimity's experience, once seduced by her lashes, no man was a good enough actor to play the innocent with such aplomb. Besides, if he'd been conscious of his betrayal (during or after) he would never have admitted to her his meeting the Prussians in the first place. After all, the whole initial encounter had occurred at a gentlemen's club, and those were notoriously difficult to crack. Gentlemen's clubs were far better at keeping secrets than the government.

So when Dimity eventually managed to extract herself, still tea-less, it was to report to the War Office that the Prussians had most certainly managed to steal or at least learn something significant from Professor Meeld-Forrison, but that the man himself was unaware of this fact. Her assessment being that the poor man was shy but innocent, and might best be guided into studies with less dangerous applications.

Dimity also departed having learned Professor Meeld-Forrison's opinion on every breakfast item offered unto the great British public, tea notwithstanding, and attained what she thought might be her twenty-second offer of marriage.

Really, being a spy could be too tiresome. She thought, not for the first time recently, that it might be time for her to move on from the work. Perhaps the next mission would be her last. Maybe she should accept one of those marriage offers. Except there was only one man she actually wanted to marry – and he was difficult.

Lord Pritchard was waiting for her just outside the laboratory, in the guise of her uncle and guardian, indulging in his niece's peculiar interest in science. He was her safety on this mission – not that she needed one, but the War Office always insisted.

Lord Pritchard was an elderly military gentleman with firm opinions on the delicacy of proper feminine behavior and therefore thought Dimity was *wonderful*. Men of his sort always did. When she expressed her need for sustenance, he took her to Lottapiggle Tea Shop on Cavendish Square, because it was the best in town, and a young lady of her sensibilities must have the very best.

Dimity agreed with him, of course, and then wondered if he might be convinced on the matter of small gifts of jewelry to the most holy paragon-ness of feminine behaviors, *viz*, herself. Then thought better of it.

One shouldn't really confidence-trick one's co-workers, should one?

Sometimes it was difficult to stopper up her training. But then, Lord Pritchard was so very set in such disagreeably old-fashioned ways, and so very rich, and he *would* keep telling her she ought to give up her wild ways, marry, and become a proper woman, as though she wasn't perfectly brilliant at her job. To be honest, Dimity resented his instructing her to do something she was already contemplating, because she did want a husband and family and she didn't think there was anything wrong with that. It was simply his tone and the way he said it, all patronizing. Perhaps she should fleece him for a small diamond bracelet or two, simply for revenge on the universe for having to put up with him.

Dimity had her tea, ignored her dining companion, and fantasized about leaving off the intelligence game. She fully intended to organize a husband for herself eventually. She had always rather admired the simple life – it was only that her dearest friends tended to be active in the world of espionage, someone had to keep an eye on them, and she was made loyal. Still, Dimity was resolved to settle down in the countryside with a nice gentleman someday. This gentleman had once been rather an amorphous idea. But now, well, *now* she had her eagle eye set on someone particular. Unfortunately, the chap was under the startling bad impression that he did not like her. He was obviously mistaken, and she would fix his misconception forthwith.

You see, Dimity had always believed that an engagement, especially one's own, ought to be carefully constructed, especially when the gentleman in question was both unaware and unwilling. It was possible that she might have to kill someone to convince him. But she was hoping she could get away with a mild maiming. Dimity wrinkled her nose in thought. Then again, he was awfully stubborn.

All of which was to say, she certainly didn't need sainted Lord Pritchard's advice on the matter.

She sipped her tea. Lottapiggle really did very good things with the sacred leaf.

She looked at Lord Pritchard through thick dark lashes. Dimity had *powerful* lashes and she always used them to good effect.

"You wouldn't mind one more tiny stopover before we head back, would you, my dear lord?"

"Not at all, poppet."

While jewelry might be asking a bit much, there were other accessories to consider. Dimity twinkled at him. "It's only that there are these *charming* gloves I've had my eye on for ages. Of course, they didn't have my size. I've been waiting for the smaller ones to come in. My hands are so very delicate, you see." She brushed her white fingers seductively against the handle of her teacup. They were beautiful and creamy, if she did say so herself. Dimity actually had done quite well in her fingersmith and lock-picking classes. A girl had to take care of her hands if she wanted to delve smoothly into pockets. She soaked hers in cream most evenings.

Lord Pritchard gleamed at her. "We must protect such beauties, of course, pretty poppet. I'm sure the War Office can wait for your report."

Dimity lowered her lashes again, nibbled a biscuit, and smugly wondered if she might get *two* pairs of gloves out of the man.

It was a little too easy. Lord Pritchard was awfully susceptible to wiles. She'd have to warn Bertie of that. The boss ought to keep an eye on this man. Pritchard was weak in the face of womanhood, and if he was susceptible to her, he was susceptible to other ladies outside the War Office.

Unlike some of the other muscle they assigned to guard her back. Unlike Sir Crispin.

Sir Crispin would *not* be manipulated. She'd never managed to extract a single cup of tea out of that man, let alone a pair of gloves. It was extremely vexing, and highly attractive, of course. When she lowered her lashes at Sir Crispin, the bally fellow simply gave her one of his swarthy glowers and reminded her that he *had sisters* and anything she tried would be held against her.

Dimity wished he would hold himself against her. But if his response to the merest smile was a sardonic arched brow or a sniff of disgust, what was a young lady of tricky inclinations to do? How was Dimity to net the man of her dreams when he was as highly trained as she, and apparently capable of total resistance?

A quandary.

Plus, he kept getting other missions. Going off and looking after *other* intelligencers, when he ought to be looking after her, and only her.

It was extremely aggravating.

Dimity sighed into her tea. She hated it when men got complicated. They were so very bad at it.

CHAPTER TWO

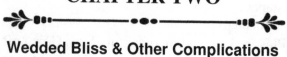

Wedded Bliss & Other Complications

Crispin and Bertie rose to their feet as one.

The entirely fabulous fellow sashayed into the conservatory with a flourish designed to encourage awe, if not outright applause. He was dressed in a manner decades, perhaps even centuries, out of date, and yet he managed to look entirely *à jour*. The man sported tight satin britches and a long brocade jacket in matched purple hues, a queue of silky blond hair tied back with a ribbon, and shoes with buckles on them. It was as if he were starring in a play, something scandalous yet much admired behind closed doors.

Cris had never met him, but he knew at once who he was. And more importantly, he knew *what* he was.

The vampire's voice was a musical tenor and rather loud for such a small person. "Bertie, *darling*, you repainted your door! I might have worn something different had I known. This outfit clashes horribly. Why did you not warn me? The very act of my walking inside surely seared the eyeballs of all who observed. Send a card 'round next time you redecorate, do, *sweetling*. What are you collecting now? Still cactuses? I suppose we all must have hobbies." He swept the room with a piercing gaze and (for lack of any additional seating) moved to perch on the edge of the table next to the tea tray, at which he glanced with mild distaste.

Cris and Bertie resumed their seats.

"Lord Akeldama, thank you so much for joining us."

"A pleasure, a pleasure, Bertie-my-peach. And you must be Sir Crispin?" The vampire had a way of moving his hands, fluttery and distracting, like baby birds.

"Delighted to make your acquaintance, Lord Akeldama. I've heard nothing but good things. Wicked, but good." Cris opted to be as dashing and diplomatic as possible, in order to make a good impression and put the man at ease. Vampires were finicky creatures, but rumor had it that, as a rule, they favored flattery.

"All the best *things* are, of course, both wicked and good. Are you?" The vampire gave Cris a fanged smile.

Cris inclined his head. "Perhaps, but one ought to preserve some air of mystery upon first acquaintance. Don't you think?"

The vampire tittered and subjected him to careful scrutiny. He seemed to approve of what he saw because a gleam entered his eyes and Cris felt as if he were one level above an extremely appealing platter of cheese.

"My, but aren't you simply *delicious*." Lord Akeldama leaned forward. "Bertie, *dearest*, you've been holding out on me. *He* works for *you*. Thus, he's clearly innately secretive. His apparel is all grace and subtlety. Plus, he's a knight. *And* he looks like a minor Greek god. Dionysus, perhaps? He should be *mine*."

The vampire leaned even more towards Cris. "When you let that lovely dark hair grow, Sir Crispin, please tell me it *curls*?"

Cris was a little afraid the vampire might actually go for his neck. He fingered the ejection button on the deadly wooden spike that lived up his left sleeve. "Into ringlets, no less, hence my reason for keeping it short. A man of my age can't have ringlets bouncing about. Lacks *gravitas*."

"Ringlets, you say?" The vampire jerked towards him, eyes dilated.

The spike snapped out and down and Cris raised his arm fast, so the sharp piece of wood pointed at Lord Akeldama's chin.

The vampire's smile widened. "Oh, he *definitely* should be mine. You haven't any artistic ability, have you, *succulent* boy? A secret penchant for the harpsichord, perhaps? A sketchbook full of salacious nudes?" His eyebrows waggled.

Crispin knew the creature was after creative talent, a sign of excess soul and the ability to survive a vampire's bite. So, of course, Cris decided not to admit to having any artistic ability. He shook his head.

Bertie was sipping his tea and looking very bored. "Really, Lord A, you're becoming predictable."

The vampire reared back, seeming genuinely hurt. "Never. How cruel you are, Bertie-my-pearl."

Bertie rolled his eyes. "Cris is nothing if not

practical. He rowed *and* bowled for New College. He's a sportsman, my dear sir. Outdoorsy. He's even been known to gallivant about on horseback, even do a little bird watching on the side. Goes ambling through the woods voluntarily, breathing cold air and getting his boots muddy. He likes the countryside, Lord A. The *countryside*! Hopeless. Definitely not drone material."

"Pity," said Lord Akeldama, still looking at Crispin's neck hungrily. "Explains why he's so delightfully robust and rugged." The covetous gaze moved over the rest of Crispin's torso. Cris resisted a mad inclination to flex. It was nice to be appreciated, even if it was mostly as food.

"You box at White's?"

"Of course." Cris arched his brows, trying for coy. He still had the spike pointed at the vampire, though.

"Oh, put your little wooden toy away, do, *stripling*. I'm civilized. I'd always ask first. And clearly, you are not for me."

Cris kept his weapon at the ready. The vampire was still tense about the eyes, and his hands were overly still. Cris never trusted a still predator.

But it took Bertie to put the nail in the proverbial coffin. "He likes women, Lord A. You know how they say – of the female inclination?"

Lord Akeldama sighed very loudly and pursed his lips. "Now that *really* is a *pity*. Can't be influenced into experimenting?"

Now it was Crispin's turn to roll his eyes. "I went to Eton, so clearly *not*." He didn't want to be impolite to the man, but he had no intention of being either

meal or lover, and certainly not both. Sometimes even
Cris had to be a touch rude to get his point across.

"Ah, well then. What a profound tragedy. So, it's
evident that *you,* gentlemen, can do nothing for *me*.
What is it *I* can do for *you*? Or should I say, for the
War Office?"

"For the queen!" crowed Bertie, full of pride.

"Yes, *that* woman." Lord Akeldama tapped his
cheek with one fine, bone-white finger.

Mrs Bagley appeared at that juncture. She had a
solid looking, and appropriately dressed, young
parlormaid with her.

The girl stepped forward, towards the vampire.
Cris watched her demeanor carefully. He would not
want her to be coerced. But she seemed genuinely
eager.

"Bloody Mary, my lord?" offered Mrs Bagley.

The maid tilted her head to one side and pulled
down her ruffled collar to show off her white neck.

"Are you sure, Mary?" Cris asked, even though it
wasn't his place as a guest in the house.

The maid glanced at him, not lifting her head,
startled. "Oh yes, sir, it would be an honor."

Cris nodded. So long as it really was her decision.

The vampire recoiled only slightly before
recovering his equanimity. "No, thank you, dearest
madame, I just ate."

The maid looked disappointed. Mrs Bagley looked
like Mrs Bagley.

Cris sheathed his spike, a little embarrassed now to
have brought it out at all. Had that been too rude?

The two ladies left.

Lord Akeldama and Cris turned expectantly to Bertie.

Bertie showed his hand at last. "Baroness Ermondy, queen of the Nottingham Hive, has sequestered herself alone in—" He paused and cleared his throat. "A, erm, damp limestone cave."

"A limestone cave, you say? How *extraordinary* of her. Do go on." The vampire seemed genuinely enthralled.

Cris watched their visitor's reactions with interest while Bertie continued.

"Her vampires are unsupervised, her household is in disarray, her servants have fled."

"Going to Goth, is she?" Lord Akeldama's eyes had narrowed slightly and he was very, very still. Cris suppressed the mad desire to twitch like a frightened rabbit in response.

"We believe there is a danger of Goth state, yes." Bertie's face was grave.

"Are they at the *black velvet* stage yet? I hadn't heard of this! How have I *not heard* of this? Vampires going to Goth, within England proper!" Lord Akeldama rose to his feet, his hands resumed their fluttering. His outfit, Cris realized, did go very nicely with the vegetation and window arrangements of the conservatory. It might not match the door, but the vampire had dressed very well for the rest of the house.

Bertie explained, "We only learned of it recently and BUR has been keeping it under wraps. So to speak. But it appears that she has isolated herself. The hive is down to one drone and three vampires. Most, if not all, of the servants have fled. You know Lord Rashwallop died last year?"

"Terrible tragedy. What was it again?" No doubt Lord Akeldama knew, but was testing them. Crispin watched him slow blink, like a cat, and wondered if vampires had to remember to blink or if they still did it naturally, even though they were undead.

"Exploding wicker-work *Aves Galliformes* of some kind. Woven willow twigs can be so very dangerous, don't you feel? Never countenance the stuff, myself." Bertie was deadpan. The vampire wasn't going to get one up on him.

"Nor I, *dear* boy, nor I. Although it has its place. Outside, on lawns and such, in my humble opinion. Was Lord Rashwallop going mad? That was the rumor. He was by far the oldest vampire in that hive."

Bertie tilted his head. "Yes. I heard that too. War Office can neither confirm nor deny. After all, that's decidedly BUR's jurisdiction."

"I didn't know BUR dealt in wicker."

"They don't. But the Dewan has been known to dabble."

"Interesting." The vampire paused his fluttering. His sharp eyes turned to Crispin, suddenly, as if he'd only just remembered he was there. Crispin gave him a head tilt. Lord Akeldama returned a small smile. "Very interesting."

Bertie pressed on. "Yes, but beside the point."

"Oh, Bertie-*blossom*, never say you have a *point*!"

Cris had to admit he was warming to the vampire, now that the man wasn't trying to actively recruit him.

Bertie seemed to feel the need to be very clear. "So

the baroness has sequestered herself, the hive is diminished, and everyone is worried. They are fully funded. They are not known as vampires, but as local and eccentric aristocracy. They had fully integrated into the local upper classes and we had thought the hive quite stable. Now this."

Cris presumed this explanation was mostly for his benefit. As the supernatural set rarely impacted his missions, Cris paid very little attention to vampire society.

The vampire looked thoughtful. "BUR believes she might actually be headed towards the final Goth state of depressive *insanity*?"

Bertie nodded.

"Blood will flow," intoned Lord Akeldama.

"Yes, it usually does when vampires lose their willies."

Lord Akeldama gave a tiny little frown. "She's not very old. It seems precipitous for her to take the *velvet path of colorless doom* so soon."

"But with a hive that small and weak? How frayed are her tethers?" Bertie respectfully countered.

"I see your point, *sweetness*. And a very *sharp* point it is."

Cris felt it was time he asserted himself. "How long has it been since she successfully conducted a metamorphosis?"

Bertie frowned. "I don't have the hive paperwork to hand. I've collected it in the study to pass along to you, of course, to read on your way up. But I believe that would be Justice Wignall. He was turned just before the first Napoleonic War."

Crispin looked at their visiting vampire. "That's not too bad for a queen." He was guessing. Fortunately Lord Akeldama concurred, so Cris didn't feel like a complete idiot.

"No, it's not. She's clearly not *that* weak. Something dire must have set her off. Could be the death, could be something more decorative. You're right to be worried, my *sweet-Bertie-boy*. Is that what you had me 'round to ask?"

Bertie nodded. "I'd like your assessment. You're the only vampire I know capable of an honest assessment."

"Because I have no hive of my own."

Lord Akeldama didn't look as sad as Crispin would have thought when he said it. He'd thought being a vampire rove was something akin to being a werewolf loner. Such a man was packless and lonely – without family. Lord Akeldama didn't seem to see it that way. If anything, he looked almost pleased by the recognition that rove status gave him a certain objectivity and autonomy, at least so far as the government was concerned.

The vampire stood and inhaled deeply, as if taking to the stage. "I would say it all does sound rather *ominous*, my sugar plums. And anyone you might send up there is at great risk, especially if Queen Octavine *is* close to the edge. Although she has a fondness for athletic young men with aggressive jawlines, so you're in there." He gave Cris a sly finger wag.

Cris, of course, admitted to nothing.

"It could be something more simple. A swarm

might be imminent?" Bertie pressed, hope in his eyes.

Lord Akeldama gave nothing back. "A vampire separating herself from life and sustenance is never a good thing, my *lovelies*. We are social creatures. Something is gravely wrong. Remember, vampires usually take out their atonement on others, regardless of fault. Nottingham is in danger."

A dramatic pronouncement from a dramatic vampire. Still, Crispin couldn't help but shiver. For BUR to be worried was one thing. For the War Office to be activated was another. But for a vampire to confirm that there was cause for concern suddenly made everything feel more pressing and dangerous.

"And now, my *darlings*, this has been *terribly* entertaining, but I must be off. There's this new play I'm simply *dying* to see." He tittered. "Well, I *would* be *dying* to see it, if I weren't already *dead*. Bertie, *sweetling*, a pleasure, as always. And Sir Crispin, you *tasty, tasty thing* you, delighted to make your acquaintance. We must meet again sometime soon. Invite me to watch you box sometime, do."

With which the vampire swept out of the room in grand fashion, presumably intent on seeing himself out.

Cris stood and followed him. Watching to make certain he entirely left the house. Vampire hearing was not to be discounted – at least, that was what he'd always been told.

He returned to Bertie once he'd ensured that the only person likely to eavesdrop on them was Mrs Bagley.

"That was unexpected."

"Crispy, darling, *that* was Lord Akeldama. He's like being suddenly doused with a bucket of warm, delicious gravy."

Cris could play this game with Bertie if he needed the distraction. "Gravy, hm? Salty, smooth, and tasty, yet profoundly uncomfortable and you're bound to need a great deal of clean-up afterwards?"

"Exactly." Bertie was still sitting and had poured himself a fresh cup of tea.

Cris was never going to be good at being still. Bertie was right to accuse him of being an active, sporty sort of chap. Since he was up already, he began to pace around the seating area of the conservatory in tight concentric circles.

"This is outside my expertise, Bertie. You know that. Send me in to fix a human household and all will be well in a heartbeat. Off to a house party with the gentry, and in a day I'll return knowing everything about everybody and having set them all to rights. But *vampires*, Bertie? And crazy ones at that. And *Sparkles* – you really want to send her into this level of mess?"

"She's our best option. High society is her bailiwick. Vampires are nothing if not high society driven, even the crazy ones. Plus, we've got her an entrée under one of her more established identities."

"The artist?"

"Exactly. A hive is always courting new drones and has the funds to do it. So we started a correspondence with the praetoriani, Lord Finbar, on Dimity's behalf. Said she was interested in viewing one of the hive's paintings, inquired as to whether the hive would consider putting it on loan to a museum collection. Dropped hints that she's a painter herself. Also showed she had organizational capacities, and might be good as a housekeeper. Finbar was instantly intrigued, suggested she come up to visit, bring some of her artist friends, and see the painting in person. And ta da, we have an invitation!" Bertie's grin was wide and full of guile, as though he had accomplished something quite profound.

"I don't like it, Bertie. Did you see Lord Akeldama's reaction? I mean really see it. He's not happy about their condition. He thinks they're doomed. He was only being halfway flippant. I'm sure his normal state is entirely flippant." Crispin's heart was doing funny things. This was worse than anyone was letting on and it wasn't like Bertie to lie to him, not when he was sending him into a sticky situation. And yet there was something here. Something Bertie wasn't telling him.

"No one is happy about Nottingham, Crispy. That's why we're sending her."

Cris nodded, yet there were still prickles on his spine.

Bertie pressed, "So you'll go as her safety?"

Cris was an adjunct safety. He'd been knighted for his services to the Crown after a particularly horrendous military action. He was not an indenture. The War Office couldn't order him into anything, they could only request his services. Once he said yes, *then* they could order him about. He worked for them because he liked to be useful, and he wasn't sure he was good for anything else. Also, he needed to make things right, make things better. For everyone, he supposed, even vampires. Bertie knew that about him and wouldn't want him feeling coerced or pressured.

Perhaps that was why his friend was hiding something.

Cris continued his pacing, turning on his heel every six steps, rhythmically, making a satisfying squeak on the marble floor. "Let me understand fully. You want us inside quickly to determine the ramifications of the hive's situation. Then Sparkles is to tidy up if she can, and I'm to get her out fast if she can't. Because she'd want to stay and fix everything, if there's even half a chance of saving them, at risk to her own life."

"Got it in one, my dear chap."

"What happens if we fail?"

Bertie looked away, the intensity of his dark, sharp eyes elsewhere, hiding the truth.

Cris pressed. "Bertie, what's the plan to safeguard our retreat?"

"BUR will send in a sundowner."

Cris paused, shocked. "For only the queen, or..."

Bertie wouldn't look at him.

Crispin's skin prickled all along his hairline. "Kill an entire hive? That's slaughter!"

Bertie's smiling mouth turned down. "We can't let a hive go fully Goth, old chap. The last time that happened, France had a revolution. The white wolf walked and thousands died."

"How long do Sparkles and I have to save them?"

"Two weeks."

Cris ran both hands through his short hair, tugging it, using the pain to center himself and to stop the prickling. "You don't ask for much, do you?"

Bertie stood and faced him, swallowing, chin firm. Bertie his boss at the War Office rather than Bertie his friend. "So, Sir Crispin, I'm formally requesting – will you take the mission?"

A gentleman's word is his bond. Cris glared at Bertie. "Of course I'll bally well take it. Someone has to keep an eye on her. Someone has to save the hive. I guess it's us. Curses, how has BUR let it come to this?"

"They've had a lot of werewolf problems recently."

Cris puffed out his cheeks, then let the air out in a huff and began to pace again. It occurred to him that he'd been short with one of his oldest friends. A man who'd put up with him since university. Bertie, who had never minded where Cris came from, how awful his father was, even when other families instructed their sons not to associate with "that Bontwee boy." Bertie, who'd seen him through bumbling awkwardness and broken hearts. Who'd stuck by him for years now.

"I'm sorry, old chap, I didn't mean to be curt with you." He sighed and ran his hands through his hair again. "Honestly, Bertie, how am I supposed to pretend to be an artist? I'm neither an intelligencer nor an actor."

He gestured at himself.

There was no doubt about it, he was a sporting fellow – big boned and far too tan, and there were some who called him *rangy*. Rather unkind, that. It wasn't as if he played golf. Still, pale, wispy artistic type he most definitely was *not*. Not that all artists leaned that way, as a rule, it was simply that he didn't even begin to look the part, and in espionage it was best to activate expectations, erroneous or not.

Bertie sighed. "We will give you clothing with paint splotches on it. Try to slouch a bit. Let your hair grow." He squinted at Cris, as though seeing him fuzzy might improve him into an artistic inclination.

Cris crossed muscled arms over a wide chest and tilted his head at his friend.

Bertie winced. "Perhaps you're the kind of artist who does things with large sheets of metal? You know, whelping or winching, something brawny and modern like that? Or stone maybe? Great slabs of granite? We could sprinkle marble dust in your hair? You should grow a beard."

"I am *not* growing a beard, Bertie. Not even for my country."

"You do have a very manly jaw. Pity to cover it over."

"Thank you, old chap."

"How about mutton chops? Or a mustache? That'd serve double duty – save you from Lord Akeldama's interest. He's reputed to have a horror of mutton chops and mustaches."

Cris ignored this and pushed the conversation back to the mission. "And when the vampires ask me to actually create something arty?"

Bertie flicked the fingers of his free hand. "Just spend the entire visit claiming you're in the throes of a tragic creative dearth. Lament your sad state. Artists do that sort of thing, don't they? Regularly? It's like writer's block, only with paint."

Cris wrinkled his nose. "I suppose so. I don't fraternize with many artists."

"Wear ill-fitting clothes. And tilt your hat forwards all the time."

"Sometimes I hate the images you put in my head, Bertie."

"The Honey Bee will carry you."

"I'm not overly fond of *that* image either."

Bertie grinned at him.

Cris sighed, wondering how many oversized shirts he had in his wardrobe and what his valet was going to say about it all.

"When do we leave?"

"Tomorrow afternoon, by dirigible."

"Oh, I say! Not floating." Cris was not a very good floater – it played hell with his tummy.

"Floating."

"Blooming heck."

"Oh, and Crispy, you're also supposed to pretend to be married to her."

"Oh, Bertie, I say. That's not on!"

"Wedded bliss, Crispy. Your chance to try it out."

"I hate you sometimes, Bertie." Cris said it with love, of course.

"Have fun, old chap."

Cris paused at the doors to the conservatory. "I do have one artistic inclination... but if you tell anyone outside of the bounds of this operation, Bertie, so help me God!"

Bertie raised one hand. "I swear it."

So Cris told his oldest friend his second greatest secret.

Dimity bounced only a little when she saw who was waiting for her on the embarkation green. But she did most assuredly bounce – honestly, she couldn't help it. *Sir Crispin* was her safety for this mission! Someone was on her side at last! Probably Bertie.

She sent her boss at the War Office a fervent prayer of gratitude. *Thank you, Albert Luckinbill. May your cacti be fruitful and multiply.*

Dimity's truest friend in the whole wide world was a bit of a climber. Not socially – actual physical climbing, like up mountainsides. Turn your back on Sophronia for one minute and she was inching over the side of a dirigible or getting up on top of a moving train. But Dimity wasn't that kind of intelligencer. Oh, she could climb if she *must*, but it wasn't her strong suit. Nevertheless, as certain as fire opals were her favorite jewel (and they absolutely were, so colorful!) Dimity Plumleigh-Teignmott wanted to climb Sir Crispin Bontwee.

Firstly, let us be clear, he was a physically pleasing specimen of manhood. Extremely well-proportioned, with excellent musculature, a well-turned leg, and the kind of cheekbones that once would have driven Dimity into fits of poetry. Dimity no longer wrote poetry, for which the world was no doubt grateful. But *those cheekbones.* Sir Crispin also had nice straight teeth, or she believed he did. He rarely smiled, so it was difficult to know for certain. His mouth was generous and looked like it wanted to smile often – only for some reason he felt the need to keep very good control over it.

Dimity really wanted to make him smile, and tried, a lot. And failed. A lot.

Which happened to be the most attractive thing about Sir Crispin – his excellent control. For example, the man was always moving, always in motion, yet not nervous about it, simply energized. It was as though he was leashed and held tight by his own discipline, like some jungle cat ready to pounce. And Dimity wanted desperately to be the recipient of a good pouncing.

Oh dear, there she went, waxing poetic. That kind of wax would never do.

It was only that Dimity had never wanted a man to pounce on her before, but she wanted it from Sir Crispin. Had done for simply ages. Yet he resisted all her wiles, most valiantly.

Lastly, Sir Crispin numbered the fact that he was a tuppenny knight. Not too high status, not too obscure, but perfectly balanced on the cusp of the nobility. Which meant he was brave and handsome, and ranked exactly as Dimity always wished. Hadn't she said, well over a decade ago now, to that selfsame truest friend in the whole world, that all she really wanted was to one day marry a tuppenny knight?

And here he was.

Dimity always liked to be a woman of her word. She wanted Sir Crispin settled, preferably in her bed, in her house, in her life. Hers.

And now, well *now*, they were about to be sequestered, together, for a fortnight, in a vampire hive. Fantastic!

To her profound delight, when he handed over her papers and her identity, Sir Crispin also handed over a wedding ring... they were to be sham married as well!

Dimity couldn't help it. She grinned at him. "Well, good evening, *husband*."

Sir Crispin heaved a great sigh. "Sparkles."

"This ring is not to my taste." It was a sad, plain little thing, no real splash to it.

"Next time I'll insist Bertie provide a much bigger, more elaborate statement. But we are meant to be poor starving artists, remember?"

"How can I distract someone by fiddling with it, when it boasts barely a single paste diamond?"

"What, those earrings aren't bold enough?" He flicked one gently, teasing.

Dimity was wearing a pair of amethyst, diamond, and silver chandelier earrings, huge and dangly and utterly fake. As a poor artist, she didn't mind that they looked it a bit too. Except the silver, of course. That was real. The design of each dangle ended in a nice sharp point that could cut flesh if applied properly and with enough force. One should always keep silver around in these days of werewolves.

Dimity swung her head so that they shimmered in the afternoon light. Sir Crispin pretended to shield his eyes in mockery of their brilliance. But his own eyes were shining at her with amusement. Oh, she did so very much like the man.

She glanced over her paperwork while they stood in the queue to board. "Mr and Mrs Christopher Carefull. Charming."

"No, *Carefull*."

She bumped him, happy for his teasing. "And I'm *Jonquil* again. Only this time the artist identity, and married now. I do like that persona. Well, Mr Carefull, shall we?"

Sir Crispin rolled his eyes. "I'm calling you *Mrs Carefull*. Or Sparkles, of course." He bent to scratch the ears of someone's pampered pup. The dog lolled a tongue at him, and Cris told him in very warm tones how *good* he was. Dimity thought Sir Crispin was awfully good too.

"And I shall call you *husband*. It suits you so well." She fluttered her lashes down at him suggestively. Trying to hide how much she genuinely did like the moniker.

The queue moved forwards and Sir Crispin stood to show their chits to the float conductor, who waved them aboard.

Dimity trotted ahead and up the gangplank, twirling her parasol and waggling her hips to make her cage crinoline sway as much as possible. "Come along... *husband*."

He groaned and strode after her. Catching up easily and poking her with his arm. Which she then grasped as if he had offered it quite gallantly.

She gave him a coy glance. "Such a gentleman I've married."

"You're not going to let this slide, are you?" He was so careful with her, always, even when teasing. Almost shy about it. Dimity had always felt, from the very beginning, that there was something odd about Sir Crispin. She had realized eventually, almost too

late, the fact that he was a genuinely good man. And
there were so few of those about. She'd almost missed
it. Almost missed him.

"You could call me *wife*, you know." She wanted
to hear it in his voice.

He remained stoic. Such a difficult man. "This
way, *Mrs Carefull*."

"Don't mind if I do, *husband*."

"*Carefull* of the step up on to the deck." He was
almost smiling. His expression fell, however, the
moment they boarded.

The float up to Nottingham was likely to take the
better part of the afternoon. And it turned out that poor
Sir Crispin wasn't a very good floater. Dimity
intended to make the most of it. *Take every
advantage*, her teachers used to say. Dimity most
certainly would. She would dab his brow and wave
the smelling salts and boil water and all manner of
wifely caring things that she could think of.

They had a private dining berth, mostly because
they needed to discuss tactics. Otherwise the War
Office would never have countenanced the expense.
Dimity was grateful. She had a considerable amount of
baggage to keep track of and would rather it stayed
with them. Plus, it was a great deal easier not to talk in
code. And how could she be demonstrably wifely and
kind if she had to be on her guard around strangers?

The airship smelled of coal smoke and orange
blossoms. It was not unpleasant. And they enjoyed an
easy launch and puff up, despite Sir Crispin's
clutching the berth cushions like some maiden aunt on
her first air venture.

Much to Dimity's disappointment, he didn't seem to get very airsick. Not that she wanted him sick, but she simply didn't often get the chance to be a ministering angel. It seemed more that he was afraid of heights, which frankly, Dimity couldn't do much about except try to distract him with chatter or irritation or both. Also wifely, but not in the way she really wanted to prove she could be. Not worthy. Just her normal manipulative self.

After bringing them tea, the onboard footman left them to their own devices. Dimity stared out wistfully at the puffy clouds and the countryside below, chattering away about how frustrating the inventor had been on her last mission. This seemed to work well enough, as Sir Crispin became increasingly irritated by her descriptions of her attempted seduction (she could understand, she'd been frustrated herself) and eventually distracted himself from their great height by securing the berth for maximum privacy.

England was a patchwork of green below them. Dimity sighed in pleasure and poured the tea. She did miss floating. Such a civilized way to travel.

Sir Crispin, on the other hand, was finally looking slightly green. Assured that they could not be overheard, and that Dimity did not want the window sash up, he sat down with a groan.

"Why must we bob about in such a vulgar manner?" he grumbled.

Dimity smiled at him, wishing she had dimples. Surely even Sir Crispin couldn't resist a dimple. "My fault, I'm afraid. I insisted. I can't abide trains. I had a nasty experience crashing one as a girl. Are you well? Should I ask the steward for a cold cloth to lay upon your brow?"

"No thank you. It's my normal process when floating. Abject infantile terror, illness, and then resignation. I shouldn't like to inconvenience the steward." He seemed more disgusted with himself than the situation warranted.

"My dear sir, not everyone can be a good floater. And I assure you I, not the steward, would dab your forehead in a wifely and winsome manner."

"I'm sure you would be very winsome about it, but I don't want to put you out, either. I assure you I'll be fine. Resignation will happen soon enough."

"Pity." Dimity glanced down at the dossier they'd been given. Mostly in cipher, of course, although nothing too sophisticated. It was only the government, after all. Dimity decided that she'd demand a tour of the dirigible's boiler room before they depuffed, and dispose of them safely then. First she'd memorize what was needed, of course, and prove her acumen to Sir Crispin.

"What concerns me," said Dimity, into the only slightly awkward silence of their both reading about vampires, "is the condition of this supposed cave the queen has sequestered herself in. I mean to say, what kind of cave is it? Is there hot and cold running water? Air ventilation? Heating? Not that vampires care much for heating, but you must see my point? There's a matter of serious concern when a *cave* is in play."

"It is Nottingham. There's basic plumbing in any given cave of any respectability."

"Oh, a *respectable* cave, is it? Where does it say that?" Dimity blinked at him (unintentionally, for a change). "Unless... Is Nottingham very much known for its respectable caves, then?"

"Most assuredly. Whole ruddy town is riddled with them. Most grand houses boast a cellar of some kind carved into the limestone. There's a vast network of interconnected underground pathways and such. All built by vampires and their minions, of course, during the Dark Ages. They were forced underground, you see? Werewolves took to Sherwood Forest, started robbing noblemen, inventing ridiculous nicknames for themselves, and gallivanting about in overly tight hosiery. But the vampires, they went underground."

"Gracious," said Dimity, "I'd no idea. I mean to say, I'd heard about the Sherwood werewolves, of course – who hasn't? Didn't they wear hoods with feathers in, or some such rot? – but not the vampires."

"Isn't that often the case?"

Dimity nodded. One was tempted to think of vampires as more flashy than werewolves, but the werewolves were usually more bold – an interesting dichotomy. She evaluated Sir Crispin from under her lashes. He'd make a good werewolf. That wide chest and deep, gentle voice. She tried not to hum in appreciation.

She pulled herself away from manly chests and the idea of Sir Crispin in tight hosiery gallivanting through forests (because that was near to restarting her inclination for verse). "So a city of caves and, we hope, plumbing. Now, do we have a tactic for me to deploy within the hive? Seduction? Is it a matter of redecoration? Or am I to focus on matchmaking and relationship management?"

"Possibly all three." Sir Crispin looked none too pleased by this idea.

"Let's discuss seduction first."

He looked even less happy. "If we must."

Sir Crispin didn't want her seducing others, did he? That was interesting. Very interesting indeed. Perhaps there was forehead dabbing and tight hosiery in her future after all. Nevertheless, she did have a job to do. She couldn't take Sir Crispin's sensibilities into account, much as she might enjoy it. "Would the youngest member be the most susceptible to my wiles, do you think?"

Sir Crispin shook his head and slid over the file on Justice Wignall. "Mr Wignall is not recommended. He's of the Lord Akeldama persuasion and rather flighty, lots of handkerchiefs. There are rumors of long white night-rails and pretend fainting fits."

"Oh dear," Dimity shook her head gravely. "Definitely not susceptible. Can't have two people in a relationship, both of whom rely on strategic fainting. What about this Lord Finbar?"

"He is a good target. So is Lord Kirby. Both are very old-fashioned, as you might expect from non-London vampires. And we all know you're good with an old-fashioned gentleman."

"I am." Dimity wasn't going to deny praise from Sir Crispin, even when he said it as though it annoyed him. "Do we have a preference?"

"Lord Finbar is hive praetoriani and the one you've been corresponding with. Well, the one the War

Office has been corresponding with on your behalf. There are copies of the missives for you to review at the back of the stack, see there? He'll be quite agitated after prolonged separation from his queen, since apparently she has refused to see all but one drone for many months. I think he's the weakest link. So..."

Dimity wasn't thrilled about having to go the seduction route. Not in front of Crispin – not when she'd rather seduce *him*. And not for what she was hoping was her final mission. Seduction was overdone as a rule – she'd like something a bit more challenging. Still, if everyone thought this was the best approach... "Don't seduce the hive's one remaining drone, then? Human targets are usually preferred. Less experience."

"No, definitely not him." Sir Crispin's face took on a peculiar expression. "He's high risk."

"You're worried that on him, seduction would be *too* effective?"

"Yes, I am." He was looking twitchy, as though he wanted to pace. Also less green and more annoyed. His dark eyes were almost sparking with irritation. "I'm worried it would be too effective on Finbar as well. And Kirby."

Dimity hid a grin. Was that envy she sensed, or some more affectionate need to protect her than mere safety? Either way, it spoke to hidden feelings and she liked that idea very much. Perhaps Sir Crispin didn't see her as completely frivolous. Perhaps he even enjoyed her company more than his near constant frown and forced politeness would suggest.

She gave him a tentative opening. "You prefer a redecoration and household management approach?"

He gritted his teeth, and bounced one leg up and down. "Of course I do. But policy dictates seduction first."

Dimity nodded. "It's usually the most effective tactic."

"With you, of course it is."

"Sir Crispin! What a nice thing to say."

He gave her an exasperated look. "We are under a time crunch. We've only two weeks before BUR comes crashing in."

Dimity sighed. She didn't like to be under pressure like that, and she hardly saw what good BUR thought they could do. "I think the household approach might work too, depending on what drove the queen underground. I mean, if we could bring it into the modern age, make it beautiful, make *them* beautiful, she might be tempted to return above ground. Vampires do love beautiful things above all else. Except perhaps human blood."

Sir Crispin nodded. There was no rehash needed, although they had been instructed to try seduction first. So that's what she would do, like it or not.

Dimity flipped through to read the description of the Nottingham Hive's only surviving drone (whom Sir Crispin hadn't yet met but already didn't like). Cinjin Theris, actor. *Oh my.* She read on. Multiple affairs. Men and women. Possibly even a werewolf or two. "Goodness me! This drone seems delightfully salacious. Highly sexed young gentlemen with delusions of stage talent are some of my favorites. So full of pride and so easy to manipulate because of it. I once entertained starting an occult recruitment movement, collecting them for a *cause* of some kind. They're so impressionable and there are so very many of them in London these days. Then I realized, that's what werewolves are for. And, honestly, do I have the time to spearhead a cult? I ask you. No, I do not."

Sir Crispin was staring at her in a sort of awed disgust. "The working of your mind is a thing of great beauty and profound horror."

"Why, thank you. What a nice thing to say!" Dimity was thrilled.

"You see? Now, where were we?" Sir Crispin looked at her with a fond exasperation this time, but his leg had stopped bouncing up and down.

Dimity reiterated the decision. "Lord Finbar for the approach? Redecoration as a backup plan."

"Agreed. Now, shall we get on with our memorizing?" He settled back, a map of Nottingham in his lap, bent on studying the layout of the town. As any good safety would.

"Yes indeed." Dimity collected her paperwork, glancing over it one final time to be certain she hadn't missed anything. She read the letters she was purported to have written very carefully, wincing a bit at the grammar. *No serial comma, really?* What did they take her for? An artist might be a tad lax in her missives, but to drop a comma? How ghastly.

Finally, she finished to her satisfaction and waved the stack at Sir Crispin. "Are you done with these?"

"I am, thank you."

"I shall dispose of them then, shall I?" She tied them up with a bit of string and tucked them under one arm.

"Going to demand a tour of the boiler room from the airship steward?"

"Of course I am."

"Of course you are."

CHAPTER THREE

In Which There Are Pointy Bits

Fortunately for Cris, his airsickness wasn't overly debilitating. He suspected it was partly rooted in abject terror. Not illogical terror – if you asked him, it wasn't natural to be up so high. A chap was born and died on solid ground and not meant to spend time hovering above it, if he was lucky. Fortunately for his heart, the float was remarkably calm. The aetheric current that they hopped northwards, just inside the gray, was pleasingly sedate. Cris was delighted. Nothing would be worse than to be sick in front of his Sparkles.

Dimity returned to the dining compartment some hour or so later, the steward very much *at her disposal* and all incriminating paperwork safely *disposed of*. The steward's face, when he discovered that Mrs Carefull did indeed come attached to a Mr Carefull of Crispin's dimensions, was crestfallen. Then, when he heard Dimity cry, "Husband, I missed you. I do so hate to be parted from you for even a moment," he looked like he might weep. Cris actually felt sorry for the poor blighter. He slipped him some coins in recompense and gave him a sympathetic smile.

Dimity collapsed next to him, not across from him as was proper, and smiled coyly, cheeks flushed from wandering the dirigible. She looked glowing, and relaxed, and pleased with herself. He shifted, uncomfortable.

Unfortunately for Cris, a lock of hair seemed near to escaping her elaborate coiffure. He was weak in the face of it, and was reaching forwards before he realized it, to tuck it back up under her hat.

Her smile deepened and she nudged into his hand expectantly. So he cupped her absurdly soft chin, annoyed at his lack of self-control, even as he told himself he was only practicing for the marriage show and that others might still be watching.

The door clattered as the steward closed it ostentatiously behind him.

Cris kept touching Dimity.

Dimity's hazel eyes had flecks of green in them. It was rather extraordinary. And her lashes were ridiculous – no wonder she employed them so readily.

"Tell me, Sir Crispin—"

"You'd better start calling me Cris, at least from here on out."

"Oh really, may I? How delightful."

"It's the name, remember? We're Mr and Mrs Christopher Carefull."

Her face shuttered only briefly. She had excellent control and pulled it back immediately. He, of course, was annoyed by how much he enjoyed that brief chink in her facade.

She pressed on. "So, I'm to be an aspiring painter of indifferent watercolors." She pointed to the corner, where a portable self-folding easel and a stack of pressed paper resided. Some of the paintings were finished, some not, and all were carefully packed in a large leather portfolio.

"Indeed." Cris nodded. "And *are* you an indifferent watercolorist?"

"Highly indifferent, I assure you. But I've enough facility to pass for raw, untrained skill to a hungry vampire. Even though I know, and so does anyone of lengthy exposure, that I've no actual talent to speak of."

"No, your talents lie elsewhere, don't they?"

Dimity tilted her head towards him, earrings swaying. "Do they? Are you certain of that, *husband?*"

Crispin's throat went dry. "No, but I suppose we will be sharing a bed for the next fortnight."

She blushed at that. Even she couldn't entirely control blushes. He nodded internally. So not as experienced as she was wont to pretend. He would be stalwart and treat her with nothing less than complete respect and gentility – the looming spectre of his father's lascivious treatment of young women making him shudder and pull back.

She looked slightly hurt at his recoiling, then brightened. "Oh, is your airsickness returning? Do you need a cold compress? Should I dab your fevered brow?"

He almost shammed indisposition to give her a reason to dab, she seemed so excited by the prospect. After all, that meant she'd be close and touching him, and who was he to muck with the inclination? He didn't, in the end, but he definitely considered it. Then he realized that was exactly the kind of thing his father would do – take advantage of the chit's goodwill – and felt like a cad.

"My brow, I assure you, can remain undabbed," he said, perhaps a bit curtly, annoyed with himself.

Dimity nodded and settled back and away from him. She nibbled her lip. "So what is *your* artistic skill on display then, *husband?*"

Cris felt himself flush. He was grateful for a certain never-talked-about ancestor who'd gifted his family a dark complexion, himself in particular. He'd been teased at school for being swarthy. Until he'd grown into his shoulders and taken up boxing. He cleared his throat. "I believe they have let it be known that I, erm... That is to say, I have no little capacity for, uh, not to put too fine a point on it... dancing." He almost whispered the last.

"What? You mean to say, ballroom and the like?"

"Yeeessss..."

"There are further terpsichorean pursuits for a man of your position?"

"And, erm, ballet."

Dimity's hazel eyes went very big indeed. "Ballet! Ballet? With pointy feet and fluffy skirts and dramatic collapses? And the waving arms above one's head like a spring breeze and *everything?*"

Cris rolled his eyes at her. "Yes, Sparkles, pointy feet and *everything*. I never performed, of course – too much a soldier to take to the stage. But when our childhood dance instructor discovered I had the acumen, and with six sisters, all of whom number grace as their only saving grace, so to speak, ballet seemed a natural progression. Once we learned all the quadrilles we could muster, he had us leaping *and* twirling."

"Twirling, you say?"

"Yes. *Twirling*." Cris tried to keep his voice as bland as humanly possible. "Even the occasional pirouette."

Dimity angled herself next to him, presumably so that she could stare up into his face in delighted awe. "And what happened next?" She smelled faintly of milk and honey and rosewater, like a French pudding of refined delicacy.

"Father came home early and put a stop to the dance master, but too late. The ballet had already taken. It's actually proved quite useful over the years. Surprisingly broad applications, ballet. Improved my bowling arm no end. Helped me master fencing *and* fisticuffs. After all, no one expects a pirouette. Especially not in battle."

Dimity's face went slack with carefully hidden amusement. "Especially not from a man of your stature?" She gestured with her chin at his broad frame.

"Exactly."

"Interesting secret weapon you have there, my knight."

"Stop it, Sparkles."

She sniffed and returned to the mission. "At least you have barterable skills for drone status. We should make an appealing pair. I intend to gently indicate some difficulty conceiving children and with the marriage bed, as well. To make us, you know, more *tempting*."

Everyone knew vampires did not recruit breeding humans. Went against nature, that did. One didn't pot about with one's food supply.

Of course, Cris nearly said, "*Do* you have any troubles in that arena?" as revenge for her teasing him about the ballet. But he stopped himself because all upbringing to the contrary, he wished to be gallant, not crass, and Dimity was still a lady, for all her worldly ways and ready quips.

Instead, he turned his jaundiced eye on the veritable mountain of additional baggage his so-called wife had brought along in addition to the leather portfolio of indifferent watercolors.

"Really, Sparkles, are we not supposed to be *artists*, suffering pecuniary struggles and eschewing material concerns in pursuit of a higher spirit of creativity?"

Dimity pouted at him.

He wanted to nibble that sticking-out lower lip. No doubt she would taste as sweet as the honey of her moniker.

"Well, yes, but I've never been to Nottingham before. And I've never infiltrated a vampire hive before, either. I mean to say, will there be social events? Do I need a ball gown? How many ball gowns? I don't ride, but Nottingham is the countryside, so I had to pack a riding habit. Then there's my small crossbow with the wooden bolts, not to mention enamel-inlaid muff pistols to consider. Then once I had muff pistols, I had to include muffs, because surely it gets cold up north? And I thought, foxglove – is it indigenous to the area? And would I have time to make poison if I needed it? So I packed some ready-made, to be on the safe side. And then, well, if I'm taking digitalis, why not throw in a little arsenic and some cyanide? And then I thought perhaps werewolves might be involved, so I added a few bottles of silver nitrate and a silver letter opener. I was only going to bring a few, mind you, but suddenly I felt my entire apothecary case might be necessary. And frankly, if I'm bringing the ball gowns, matched jewelry is also quite, *quite* necessary. Before you ask, I do need all five jewelry cases – you don't call me *Sparkles* for nothing, now, do you? And if I'm packing the poison rings, there are bladed fans to consider, and hats with garrote ribbons, and heat-resistant reticules, and in the end—" She finally paused for breath. "I packed the whole of this season's wardrobe, and all associated accessories, even the deadly ones." She tilted her head. "Especially the deadly ones. I mean to say... *vampires*."

"Very perspicacious of you," said Crispin, because really, what else could he say? "I begin to think espionage is merely an excuse for advanced accessorizing tactics."

"Can you think of a better reason? I also packed the very latest fashion papers out of Paris. Did you know *bustles* are the next *de mode* on the horizon? I never would have believed it. In my lifetime... bustles? I mean to say, what's next, a bum roll?"

"What's a bustle?" Cris asked, confused.

Dimity put her hand to her chest, pressing against

the brooch at the ruff of her carriage dress. "What's a bustle? What's a bustle! You ignoramus!"

Crispin never pretended to be more than a man of a soldiering mindset. If he could wear his uniform for all time and never think about proper attire, he probably would. He disliked making such decisions and left his toilet and dress entirely up to his valet. He supposed, as a starving married ballet dancer without staff, his sham wife would be dressing him forthwith. No doubt Dimity was up to the task.

"I don't follow the fashion papers," he confessed, without shame. "And bustles have yet to come up at my club."

Dimity giggled. "I certainly hope they don't come up at your gentlemen's club."

"So, what *is* a bustle?" He was intrigued now.

"That's for me to know and you to admire later."

He shifted a bit, slightly concerned for the state of his trousers if this *bustle bum roll* was what he was imagining it was. Some foundation garment perhaps, light and filmy, floating around Dimity's slim legs and flared hips and round... Could such a thing be depicted in fashion papers, and how could he get hold of the ones she'd brought to find out? And would Dimity wear one for him, without much else, if he asked very nicely?

Then he hated himself for such thoughts. He was trying to be a better man and yet around this woman, his mind would keep sinking gutter-side.

Unaware of his heated looks and stiffening nether regions, Sparkles was affectionately regarding her mountain of trunks and suitcases, carpetbags and hat boxes. "What else is there? Oh yes, of course. Well, one or two things from Mummy and Daddy, mostly explosive. A book of Latin verse that my brother left last time he visited, and a recipe for Nesselrode pudding from my aunt, which she swears by."

"Fearful they don't have Latin verse and pudding in Nottingham?"

"One can never be sure," replied Dimity darkly.

"No sporting accoutrements?"

"Oh, dear me, no! Unless you count the riding habit? Should I have brought ice skates? It *is* the north, of course, but it's also April. Have the lakes not thawed?"

Cris decided to stop teasing her. "We are visiting vampires, Sparkles. I doubt we'll even leave the house."

"What, no shopping?"

"No shopping. Worried you haven't brought enough to wear?" This was safer ground – he was accustomed to teasing his sisters about such things.

"You won't deny me *shopping* when the mood strikes. Not even you could be so very hard-hearted."

"Are you sure they have shops in Nottingham?"

"Fair point." She twinkled at him, clearly enjoying their banter.

Cris was seized by the horrible realization that he was having a marvelous time and enjoying her company immensely. And he tried so hard never to do that around Sparkles. Because everyone was susceptible to her wiles, even he, and he didn't want to be one of the enamoured crowd. He wanted to be special. He wanted to be more difficult for her. He wanted to mean something.

Pathetic, really.

Cris drew away, pressed his head back against the seat rest, stopped his natural inclination to smile back, and forced himself into calm, dour seriousness.

Dimity sighed at him. "You could relax around me a little, you know? Occasionally? I don't currently intend to slit your throat or do anything sinister."

"It's not my throat I'm worried about."

"It's not?"

"No, lower down." She blushed furiously at that and he realized that might be taken as rude, when in fact he'd meant his heart, not his prick. He struggled, wondering if he should explain. Then finally allowed her to believe he was crass. Because the other organ that might be involved was more fragile, and he didn't want to give her the slightest inkling she had any control over *that* part of his anatomy. Because she'd crush him, and wouldn't even realize she was doing it. Because along would come the next mission, and off his Sparkles would flit, to winkle his secrets out of the next susceptible male.

He'd be left behind knowing that she'd already extracted from him the fact that he was passing good at ballet. And then where would he be?

They arrived several hours after sunset, the night a gloomy one, thick with fog. Dimity was pleased it wasn't raining, as it was difficult enough to manage baggage *without* holding an umbrella. But it was colder than London, the night heavy and damp, like a cold stew. Smelled a little like wet donkey too. They were met at the Nottingham dirigible embarkation green by Lord Finbar himself, Praetoriani to Baroness Octavine Ermondy, queen of the Nottingham vampire hive. He was waiting for them outside the customs offices, sitting inside a carriage, window sash down, arms along the frame, and chin resting upon them, like some winsome schoolgirl.

In a world where it was fashionable to be very pale, because fashions were set by vampires, it was often difficult to tell a vampire from a young man of breeding. So Dimity initially thought this was someone's wastrel son, waiting on sufferance for a visiting aunt. Except that when the other passengers had been taken away by friends, family, or hired conveyance, only he was left, and he was staring at them. And he was very pale indeed. Then, deeming it safe now that the plebeians had gone, he flashed his fangs at them.

It was a bad sign that the hive had to send an actual hive-bound vampire to retrieve them. One simply didn't do such a thing. One sent servants. Therefore, the presence of Lord Finbar at the station along with a very old and run-down carriage meant there were no servants left. A vampire hive without servants was like a cake without icing sugar – functional, but not particularly nice.

The carriage was absurd, all ornate curls and finials and excessive turrets, like something out of a fairy tale. It had been retrofitted for steam and weight assist, so it had no wheels, but instead a rusty propeller attachment at the rear. It was suspended from a large black balloon.

Mounted at the front, as though it were the figurehead of a ship, was a taxidermy squirrel. The creature was pierced through the heart by a golden arrow and arranged as if in mid-leap.

"Are those cobwebs?" Dimity hissed at Cris, as they approached. "I do believe those might be cobwebs." She didn't mind if the vampire heard her – it was too shocking for words!

The carriage had once been gilt and possibly red, but someone had thought it a grand idea to paint it over black, except now the gold was peeking through at the tips and edges of all the curlicues, and the red was peeking through everywhere else. It looked like a child's toy that had been played with too often.

Lord Finbar exited the conveyance to assist Dimity inside. Or he started to, but he moved so slowly that Dimity was already in and settled by the time he recollected his civil duties. He ignored Sir Crispin entirely and did not help load the baggage (which Cris did without complaint), merely settling back into his seat and staring in gormless distraction at Dimity. Or possibly, at Dimity's neck.

Lord Finbar had a long face with sunken eyes and a mouth that could have been nicely shaped had it not been so utterly downturned. He had oily black hair combed back to show off a pronounced widow's peak.

"How do you do, Lord Finbar?" Dimity smiled as big and bright as she could.

The vampire recoiled from her. "Mrs Carefull? You're not at all what I expected from your letters."

Dimity looked down at her respectable carriage dress in alarm. She'd made sure to pick one that was older and a little worn, but she'd added a few bows and trailing ribbons in an asymmetrical manner for dramatic flair. "Am I not artistic enough?"

"That's not it at all. I thought someone less cheerful."

"One can hardly change one's disposition to meet expectations, Lord Finbar. Nevertheless, I apologize. I shall try to diminish my natural inclination to good humor. Are you well?" She continued to smile, since it seemed to unsettle him, and how much fun was that, with a vampire? Besides which, she was an artist, wasn't she – dramatic disposition, excited to be visiting a different city, pleased to meet a vampire and prospective employer.

Lord Finbar resisted her smiles. "Not at all well, not at all. The hive is suffering. Suffering most painfully. You've come to us at a grave time, very grave. Possibly literally grave, although who can know for certain? Doomed, one is tempted to think. Yes, doomed."

Dimity was taken aback. He was hardly putting any effort into recruiting her for drone status. In fact, quite the opposite. While she supposed there were some young ladies who were attracted to a certain level of Byronic melancholy, this was laying it on rather thick.

"Oh, well, it can't possibly be all that bad, can it?"

Outside, she heard Sir Crispin's warm, rumbling voice telling the porter who'd finally appeared that he would take care of her baggage. The carriage began to shake and creak as it undertook the burden of her excessive packing choices.

Apparently, Lord Finbar was only getting started. "All is crumbling into ruins. My queen is turning her back on the world of the living and the living dead. We do not sleep, we do not eat. The necks are scrawny, the pipes are dry, words wither on my tongue. All is lost and fallen into tragedy. It's like the great poets said—"

"Yes, yes, I'm sure they did say. Pipes, you mentioned? Do you mean... plumbing?" Dimity was worried. Were all her fears to be realized?

"We're flattered to have you, of course, and for your interest in our little painting," he said, finally seeming to realize she was right there, a living, breathing human artist, sitting across from him on the extraordinarily threadbare red and black brocade cushions of his carriage. "Both of you." He added, reluctantly, as Sir Crispin let himself inside and sat down next to Dimity.

As Cris closed the carriage door behind him, the entire door lost its casing and came off in his hand.

"Erp!" said Sir Crispin, straining under the weight of the thing, which might be wrought iron for all she knew.

Dimity hid a snigger with a simulated gasp of horror.

Lord Finbar merely lifted the door from Sir Crispin with barely three fingers and a weary sigh, and set it next to him on the bench as though it were a fourth passenger. He didn't even shift out of his slump.

He intoned a formal welcome with both of them sitting before him. Although his voice was so sepulchral, it was as if he were leading a eulogy. "Mr and Mrs Carefull, it is such a great honor. We have not been visited these many nights by any so vibrant and talented as yourselves. But surely you might consider turning away from us now. Will any float to your rescue, if you enter our doomed hive alone?"

Well, yes, thought Dimity. *Quite a few, I should imagine.* Cris had even mentioned that BUR would be in after them, if they hadn't managed anything substantial in a fortnight. Dimity snorted at the very idea of BUR needing to come to *her* aid. She could fix a hive in a fortnight, surely she could. Not that she thought they'd need rescuing even if she couldn't. Currently the greatest threat seemed to be excessive sentimental melodrama.

Admittedly, things could get dire if he *would* keep going on so. Dimity had experienced a romantic poet phase herself, of course. What young lady didn't? But honestly, she'd left it when she was sixteen. How old was Lord Finbar, four hundred? There was no excuse for purple elocution and aggressive morbidity at his age.

Sir Crispin shared a sympathetic look with Dimity.

He had rather lovely dark eyes, Sir Crispin did, and they were currently wide in what Dimity assumed was an effort not to burst into laughter.

Dimity privately agreed. She had met many a poet in her day. Real live ones. And opera singers. Tenors, from Italy. And not a one had laid it on as thick as this vampire.

She reached across and patted Lord Finbar gently on one bony knee. "Well, yes dear, but that seems to be putting things rather strongly, don't you think?

Can't be all that bad, can it?"

His coat – should one dignify it with that word? – was moth-eaten and, without question, made of black velvet.

Black velvet.

Dimity recoiled in horror.

He was wearing a lace cravat as well, gone cream with age, not intent. The cravat was ill tied and droopy. In fact, everything about the vampire drooped. The jacket sagged off his shoulders, the hair straggling from his head wisped against his neck, the lines from the corners of his mouth and eyes stretched downwards. Even his long face seemed to droop.

"You are, perhaps, fond of poetry, Lord Finbar?"

"I *am* a poet, Mrs Carefull."

"Oh, you are? I was under the mistaken impression that when one became a vampire one never versified again. Sacrifice of talent for immortality and so forth."

"I shall *never* give it up. Never! Even as the very act of creation is a torment. One bleeds through the pen, Mrs Carefull. Bleeds! One finds this is eternally the case, suffering for art, doesn't one, Mrs Carefull?"

Which meant he was a poet without talent. Which meant Dimity, at least, could hardly tell the difference. Still, it explained his terrible melancholy.

"Oh dear me, no, of course you shouldn't surrender your passion. I myself have a terrible weakness for a good meringue. Crispy and fluffy and chewy all at once, you see?"

He regarded her as if he thought she might be crispy and fluffy and chewy all at once. Which she supposed she probably was, to a vampire.

"Are you scribing anything profound at the moment, Lord Finbar?" she tempted him further.

"A sonnet."

"Oh yes?"

"An ode to my lost youth, my forgotten life, the crumbling of the past, the impossibility of the future, and the ruination of my dreams. It is a lyrical treatise on the passing of time, like moths through an hourglass."

"Moths is it, in your hourglass? How tiresome. I should get it cleaned, if I were you."

And so went the conversation. Fortunately, it was a blessedly quick trip from the green to the hive house. Not because the carriage was fast, but because the distance was short.

The hive house, Budgy Hall, was located in the heart of Nottingham on one of the oldest streets, next to an extremely decrepit church, overlooking said church's graveyard. Because... *of course* it was. Why be gloomy when one could go all the way into morbid? Still, it was a good address for pretend aristocrats. Well, not pretend exactly, since all hive queens were given aristocratic titles, but Budgy Hall pretended to be for eccentric *human* aristocrats.

Dimity tried not to be impressed by the consciously gothic nature of the hive's arrangements. There were even some very old oak trees looming overhead, crooked branches and prickling leaves and ominous creaking. It was all a bit much, and certainly not stylish, but they had chosen their motif and stuck with it. One had to respect that. At least a little.

Lord Finbar did not help Sir Crispin with the baggage. He only looked over the mountain stacked atop his carriage and groaned. He had supernatural strength and no reason to complain and every reason to be a gentleman and help. But he did not.

Dimity rescued her jewelry cases, and stopped a hat box from rolling into the street, and then tried to help Sir Crispin put the bags on the stoop. He frowned at her fiercely, managing even her biggest trunk with aplomb. It was very gallant and sporting of him. Dimity was delighted, of course. His arm muscles even bulged a bit under his greatcoat. Dimity had read about this phenomenon but never seen it, not in real life.

Lord Finbar and the carriage disappeared around the corner. Dimity and Cris were left standing on the stoop, in a heavy mist that was trying to become rain, smelling a musty odor of decaying mortar and moldy fabric.

"This is ridiculous," said Sir Crispin. "That man can't possibly be real."

"He's been reading *far* too much Byron."

They looked at each other. They looked at the baggage. They looked at the door.

"Do we knock?" wondered Dimity. There was a bell pull, but the cord was so frayed that with one tug it'd fall to pieces.

Sir Crispin, a man of action, knocked loudly.

They waited.

Dimity shivered.

Sir Crispin knocked again.

The door creaked open and there stood not a butler

but a chunky gentleman with long silver hair that he wore pinned half back, with ropey strands loose down each side of his round face. Dimity assumed that, given the expression of hauteur on his face, this was another of the hive's vampires. On him the pallor of an undead constitution looked sickly. He wore what amounted to medieval robes, a tailboard or whatever it was called. He even had long trailing sleeves. It was black and made of velvet, of course. It was as if he had delusions of portraying King Lear. Dimity was not best pleased by any of it.

"Oh. Yes? Who are you?" said the vampire, quite rudely.

Dimity and Sir Crispin exchanged glances.

Sir Crispin stepped forward, gave a small bow. "Mr and Mrs Carefull."

"Do you have an appointment?" He seemed somewhat angered by their presence.

Dimity tried one of her best smiles, gesturing behind them to the mound of luggage. "Oh, but we aren't paying a call. We've come to stay, from London?"

The portly vampire only sniffed at them fiercely.

Sir Crispin tried this time. "We are artists invited to visit by Lord Finbar. My wife's a painter and has come to assess one of the watercolors in your collection. I dance and we were to consider..." He paused and delicately touched his own neck with two fingers, glancing furtively around as they were still on the stoop, in public, although the street seemed mostly deserted apart from her luggage. "You know."

"Oh." The vampire nodded gravely without

looking any less angry. "Artists. Come in, if you must."

"Were you not told of our arrival?" Sir Crispin grabbed up one of Dimity's trunks and muscled it inside.

Dimity stared. More bulging.

This vampire seemed utterly disinclined to help with the luggage either, although as he was no doubt supernaturally strong, it would have been the work of moment. Dimity resented this, since it had started to rain in earnest. She very much appreciated Sir Crispin's efforts on her behalf, and what said effort combined with said rain did for his physique.

Dimity helped, despite his stern expression, and between them they got everything inside. Then they stumbled over and around the pile, as the long-haired vampire began to walk slowly away, as if he were in a wedding ceremony, presumably leading them to their room. Without checking to see if they followed. He still hadn't introduced himself, either.

They left the baggage in the entranceway and trotted after.

The house was exactly as advertised on the outside – old, worn, and decrepit. The wallpaper was stripped, the carpets threadbare, and the curtains hadn't been washed in a millennium. Out of the rain the mustiness persisted, and Dimity contemplated the saturation of the stench, wondering if it had ever been aired in its lifetime.

Dimity was terrified of touching anything, lest it break off or leave her smudged. She tried holding her skirts against herself, but the fashion was for wide crinolines, to allude to the grace of dirigibles floating about the feminine figure, so skirts were bound to touch things.

Fortunately, the grand staircase, once they attained it, was wide enough to accommodate her skirts. She had on a dove gray carriage dress with bright purple trim to protect against the dust of travel, but little could help her now because the stairs themselves did not appear to have been cleaned in the last decade.

At the top of the staircase an extremely handsome man lounged in staged dramatic aspect. He leaned against the top railing – a brave fellow. Dimity wouldn't have trusted it to hold her weight, let alone his, as he was built with operatic proportions. He had curling light brown locks, perfectly coiffed, a prominent chin, nose, *and* brow. His eyes were large and dark and speaking, in a way that suggested extensive theatrical training. He was also flushed and ruddy in a way that screamed *humanity*.

The portly vampire wafted past him with only a glance. "There's baggage wants seeing to, Mr Theris."

So *this* must be the hive's one remaining drone.

"Artists up from London, are they?" Mr Theris looked them over with a glance that was part envy, part lust, part disgust. "Don't look very artistic to me."

Not a subtle man, Mr Theris. Curious that he should be so resentful from the start. One would think that as the sole remaining drone, he would be eager to share the burden of vampire feeding and maintenance with new prospective candidates. Yet he sounded almost jealous of their presence.

"How fancy are your southern ways, then?" He waggled his eyebrows at them.

"Mr Theris, is it?" Dimity took point. This was what she did best, after all. She reached the top step and offered a dainty hand.

Mr Theris seized it with alacrity and bowed low over it. She was horribly afraid, for one moment, that he might clutch it to his breast or kiss it.

But with a quick glance at Sir Crispin, who was now looming behind Dimity, he backed away slightly. Dimity glanced under her lashes sideways. Her safety had folded his arms and was not-quite-glowering. Really, did he have to impede her progress so?

She back-kicked him in the ankle.

"Mr Theris," she tittered, gently withdrawing her hand. "The actor? How delightful."

The man instantly brightened and relaxed, looking almost schoolboyish. "You've heard of me?"

"Word of your brilliance has reached even London, I assure you, good sir."

He seemed to remember himself and came over all seductive. "Honored to hear it, Madame."

"Mrs Carefull, painter," Dimity introduced herself brightly, and then allowed a certain dismissiveness to enter her tone, "My husband, Mr Carefull. Of whom you won't have heard – he's *only* a dancer."

Sir Crispin nodded at Mr Theris.

Mr Theris tilted his chin after the vampire. "His lordship won't wait for you. Best not lose him in this wretched tomb of a house."

Sir Crispin nodded and trotted after Lord Kirby.

Dimity batted her eyes at Mr Theris. "My bags will

make their way to me eventually, won't they, Mr Theris?"

"A few might make their way to my room, Mrs Carefull. Should you like to come searching for them?"

Dimity disguised her repulsion easily – she'd been prepared for this style of man. "That would entirely depend on which ones, now, wouldn't it? Not all baggage is created equal." With which she gave his nether regions a speculative glance and waltzed past him to trail Sir Crispin down the hall.

The vampire waited for them at an off-kilter, scratched door. Behind which their room was a picture and not in the right way.

It was big enough, but cluttered with broken antiques of varying kinds. All the cushions and blankets were dusty and threadbare. There were framed and embroidered poetry samples hung on the walls, mostly Biblical, mostly exemplifying the sins of the flesh. These were complemented by thickly pigmented paintings of Greek and Roman ruins.

There was no fire in the grate and the room was glacial. Dimity supposed that vampires didn't feel the cold and the chimney was no doubt clogged. Still, it was the very opposite of welcoming.

When she placed her apothecary kit on the bed, there being no other empty surface, a puff of dust drifted upwards, illuminated by the dim light of the room's one gas lamp.

"Charming," she said, enthusiastically.

"Mmm. Surely better than what you're used to. I'll have Theris see to your trunks." He left them alone, muscling the door closed behind him.

"This place is a mausoleum." Sir Crispin poked at the bed, from which another puff of dust emerged.

"It is utterly ghastly, isn't it? I half expect ghosts to appear 'round every corner." Dimity said this knowing supernatural hearing meant they might be overheard, but there appeared to be such interest taken in appearing as moribund as possible, no doubt her feelings of horror would be taken as a compliment. They couldn't possibly be serious about this place, could they?

"Too depressing for ghosts," said Crispin, his lip curled.

"Oh, do buck up, husband darling, we're clearly in the midst of a badly written yellow-back novel of a particularly sentimental variety."

"That doesn't inspire confidence, dearest wife. For that would make me the hero of this novel, and the hero always dies in yellow-backs."

"You're sure you're the hero?"

He arched a brow at her. "Don't get all confident yourself, darling. There are always two heroines and one of them *always* dies. We don't know which one you are, yet."

Dimity giggled. "You read the Gothics, do you, husband dear?" Sometimes it was rather fun to play a character. She did like being Sir Crispin's flirtatious artist wife.

"Perhaps you will find your paintbrushes inspired by our current predicament, my sweet."

"Perhaps I shall. Do you think they'll feed us? Or will they have forgotten we eat like humans do?"

"Mr Theris apparently still lives here. They must keep some kind of kitchen running for him at the very least. Or perhaps they buy in from a local bakery. There must be some food. Somewhere."

"I'm freezing." Dimity shivered.

"I don't think it's safe to light a fire."

"I agree."

"I'll simply have to keep you warm." He said it to sound husbandly, no doubt, but he looked rather pleased about it.

Dimity was a little too pleased herself. Sir Crispin was normally so staid and reserved around her, it was nice to see him get into a role for a change. Might give her an opportunity to pry him out of that armour of his. What was he really like when he actually liked someone? And could she get him to like her?

"Shall we to bed, then?" She thought she sounded brave.

CHAPTER FOUR

Why Not Be Tidy?

Cris was already finding it an awkward business, pretending to be married to someone he actually would like to marry – including all the carnal advantages indicative of such a union. In other words, he was forced to acknowledge to himself (at the very least) that it was challenging not to touch his Sparkles as he wished, with desire, when they were sharing a room and a bed. All his noble intentions and efforts to stop himself from becoming his father were about to be tested. Because he was certain his Sparkles, for all her machinations, was still a comparative innocent and he refused to take advantage of her or the situation.

Eventually their luggage – well, Dimity's luggage – made its way to their room. Then, much to their surprise, a tray of food appeared on the floor outside their door, an offering for the weak humans. Cris brought it in, only a little suspicious, and for lack of any other clean, flat surfaces, put it on the bed. Sparkles went rummaging in her copious bags and produced a fist-sized spiky apparatus that looked exactly like two tuning forks sticking out of a crystal.

"Is that a...?"

She held up a hand to silence him. He held his tongue and watched her precise, elegant movements. Her hands were small and fine, but not thin. Concentrating and focused, she flicked one of the metal parts with a dainty white finger, waited a moment, and then flicked the other. The two prongs produced a discordant, high-pitched humming noise, amplified by the crystal. She placed the device carefully on the floor near the door jamb.

She gave him a wide, genuine smile, pleased with herself. "Harmonic auditory resonance disruptor, the very latest design. Quite newfangled, but supposed to be particularly challenging to sensitive supernatural hearing, especially werewolves. It should work on vampires as well. Muddles them enough to make overhearing a trial. Should allow us to talk in our room, so long as we keep it vibrating."

"Ingenious," said Cris, crouching down to examine it, careful not to touch. He wondered where he could get one for himself. The sound was annoying, but not being constantly on guard when in the comparative privacy of their room would be a blessing.

Dimity cleared off an old vanity and placed their supper on it. Cris rose and went to help her. The tray contained nothing even approaching palatable – two bowls of savory porridge featuring unidentifiable meat blobs that might have started life as sausage – but at least it provided sustenance. Certainly Cris had eaten worse when on campaign, and he tended to require quite a bit of fuel.

Dimity made a face, but seemed resigned and

managed half her bowlful. He worried she hadn't eaten enough, but when pressed she only shook her head.

"It's more than sufficient, I assure you. I'm neither as big nor as active as you, husband."

Cris pretended offense. "I'm sure I've no idea what you mean."

The room had a dressing chamber attached, so they each made use of it in an attempt to preserve the dignity of a working relationship. Crispin hardly knew what to do with a nightshirt, since he normally slept in the altogether, but at least his valet had known to pack something.

Sparkles emerged shrouded in a respectable muslin nightgown with ruffles at the hem and a small train. The elaborate thoroughness of the garment told him, more than anything else could, of her genuine nervousness surrounding intimate sleeping arrangements with a man. He yearned to reassure her of his good intentions, and self-control, but was at a loss as to how to do so.

Crispin's nightshirt was an ancient white cotton affair. Goodness knows where his valet had found the bally thing. He was grateful for the warmth, and its role in protecting both his and Dimity's sensibilities, but annoyed at the prospect of the darn thing getting tangled about his thighs while he slept.

Sparkles, of course, went up against her fears with flirtation. "Oh, you do have nice legs! All that dancing, I suppose?"

She was sitting on the edge of the bed and brushing her hair. This was the first time he'd seen it entirely down and it was remarkably thick and long and fluffy. Also, clearly, quite a task to brush. Apparently he was staring, because she paused, gave him a shy smile, and waggled the brush at him. "Would you?"

He swallowed hard, sat next to her on the counterpane, keeping his body loose and welcoming, and took the brush from her hand. "Turn around, then."

She did so without comment. He began pulling the brush through as gently as he could, working out the tangles and extracting forgotten hairpins – careful to keep his knuckles, where they curled around the brush handle, from touching her skin.

"How will you put it up tomorrow, without a lady's maid? I'm afraid I haven't the skill to do it for you." He tried not to lean into her rose-milk smell, stronger now, so she must have applied a skin cream of some kind.

"Oh, I'll keep it simple or even down. I'm only a poor artist, after all."

"Not down, please." Cris marveled at the softness, and took up a hank with his left hand, squeezing it gently. Her hair smelled amazing too. Like lemon, perhaps? Yes, and it was also the source of the honey scent.

She'd bent her head forward under his ministrations. He could not resist the urge to stroke her hair back with his free hand, running a finger along her cheek and neck. Realizing what he'd done, he jerked to a stop.

She shivered and turned to him, taking the hairbrush away. Her lashes were lowered and he felt like a cad.

The muslin of her nightgown wasn't thick enough to hide the fact that she was either cold or aroused. Crispin's nightshirt was likely to be similarly strained if he stood at the moment. Only his would definitely be arousal. He sighed at his own lack of control.

She had a fine figure, under the shapeless peignoir. He knew it from years of study, certainly not because the one light was behind her and her silhouette clearly visible. Curved, soft, and round everywhere she ought to be. And he shouldn't be thinking about it.

This was what came of brushing a woman's hair.

He climbed into bed.

Dimity puttered about the room a bit longer, putting away various bits and bobs, not unpacking, more making room so she might start. He noticed her shivering.

"Come to bed. It's cold and late. You can do that tomorrow." She was nervous. Good at hiding it, of course, but by nature she was a chatterer, not a putterer.

He curled his shoulders trying to make himself seem smaller and less threatening. It was not a big bed at all, and they'd be in proximity soon. He raised a knee, to ensure his continued interest wasn't evident. Didn't want to frighten her further.

Steel set her spine and she give him a glare. "Oh, very well."

She took a little sip of air and climbed under the counterpane next to him, stiff and resolute – and firmly on her side of the mattress. She also started shivering in earnest.

He cursed his fate and ceded his scruples to his need

to ensure her well-being. "Don't be ridiculous, Sparkles, we are to spend a fortnight like this. Shift over."

He stayed on his back, but looped one long arm around her and tugged her up against his side.

She stiffened further and then gave this adorable tiny mewing noise and rolled to curl tightly against him, throwing one arm over his chest and nestling into his shoulder.

"You're so warm. How are you so warm?"

He didn't bother to answer. Just lay as still as he could, so as not to scare her away. He resisted tucking her even closer. He stopped his own hand from covering hers on his chest. He tried desperately not to absorb her.

His restraint was rewarded when he felt her go boneless against him. Warmth would do that to a girl. And then her breathing became regular and deep.

He lay, wide awake, and ached at having her there, so close. Yes, his prick ached too, but the worst of the ache was in his chest, under where her arm rested. Two layers of thick cotton between them. The ugliest room in the world around them. And he ached for something he wanted and didn't deserve to have.

They didn't meet the final hive member until the next evening, after sunset. They'd both slept the bulk of the daylight away, not uncommon in a vampire hive. In the north at this time of year, sunset came early and the days were short, just as the supernaturals liked it.

Making their way downstairs, the first thing

Dimity noted was Mr Theris, entering stage left down the hallway towards what must be the kitchens. He was escorting a buxom young shepherdess-type human.

Dimity and Cris stood and watched, wondering if this were a blatant seduction or something less sinister. Or something more sinister.

Evaluation of sinisterness notwithstanding, Mr Theris and his shepherdess disappeared together and returned by the time Dimity and Cris had settled into stilted conversation in the sitting room with Lord Kirby. Dimity talked a great deal about the paintings hanging about, and enquired after the one she'd ostensibly come to see. Lord Kirby mostly ignored her. Dimity watched the young couple walking back. Surely ten minutes was too quick for a proper seduction? Not that Dimity would know for certain – but for Mr Theris to have such a reputation and to take less than twenty minutes about it seemed unlikely. And terribly uncomfortable for the lady.

The shepherdess did look rumpled. The neckline of her gown was slightly torn, and she was smiling. She was also far more pale than she had been going in.

Dimity was somewhat relieved to see a set of neat punctures on her neck – not a seduction, but a meal. There was only a small trickle of blood coming from the wounds, but it was enough to make Dimity feel faint.

She'd never liked blood, not when it was coming out of someone. It was so final and so red.

Sir Crispin gave her a concerned look and put a steady hand to her arm.

"I'm all right. I won't succumb, I promise."

"Shall we go in," Lord Kirby instructed, rather than asked. He stood and marched towards the dining room, sleeves trailing.

Sir Crispin helped Dimity to rise and escorted her to the hallway in time to see Theris letting the human nibble out the front door. The drone gave the shepherdess a handful of silver coins, a rather nice paisley shawl to cover her marks, a steak and kidney pie wrapped in cheesecloth, and a highly decorated Valentine's card, presumably full of instructions for her health.

The young lady left looking tired but happy.

"Well," said Dimity, "someone in this hive has quite the appetite."

Mr Theris noticed them then. "Her highness *must* be looked after."

Dimity exchanged a glance with Cris. The vampire queen was eating regularly. That was the first good sign they'd had concerning the Nottingham Hive. She might have retreated from the world, but she wasn't starving herself into insanity. That was *something*. The fact that she wasn't in the hive house, though, lording it over her hive-bound menfolk and generally bossing everyone around, that was still bad. Still un-queenlike.

Mr Theris's eyes flicked to where Dimity clutched Crispin's arm.

She immediately dropped said arm, as though inspired by his covetous look, and gave him a sweet smile. "Will you escort me in to supper, Mr Theris?"

The drone gave a dramatic shrug. "Sooner you be

supper than me." His tone grated. If he was unhappy with his drone status, why was he still here? Especially when everyone else had left. And why was he the only one in the hive allowed to see the queen and bring her supper? What made him so trusted by the hierarchy?

"Oh, it'll be you, still, Mr Theris. I'm nowhere near well enough known to your gentlemen vampires to be a meal this evening. My husband and I may be artists, but we are good, honest, hardworking folk and we do not offer our necks on short acquaintance, I assure you!"

"Of course you don't. Silly me. It'll be me alone again for snacking, then, always and only me," Mr Theris grumbled, but also looked smug. Was that it? Did he like having all the power and all the control over the hive as sole drone? Did he want the hive dependent upon him, and him alone?

Dimity allowed her eyes to soften in sympathy. "Yes, so sad you must be under such strain. Quite the burden of responsibility for you alone to withstand. Whatever happened to your fellow drones?"

"They've passed on to better places." Theris sounded as morose as Finbar all of a sudden.

Dimity shuddered. He made it sound as if they'd all been killed. Yet a hive never intentionally killed its drones, so that made no sense. The hive motto was always to practice restraint and never drain a human dry. Corpses did no one any good. It was not only the law, it was also a vampire's sacred oath. After all, they were proper British citizens, not monsters! Clearly the queen, at least, had control left. The shepherdess had been fine and dandy when she departed. Was one of the other vampires going mad? Had one of them drained all their food stock? Had it been Lord Finbar? Lord Kirby?

Behind her, Dimity felt Cris shift, as if ready to fight. This was something they must include in their first report. This was something they must investigate. Were the former Nottingham drones all dead? Surely BUR would have known that. The bodies. The smell.

Mr Theris resumed his poised *dramatis personae*. "Only I was strong enough to stay. Only I was good enough to remain to witness her shame. Only I! She shows only me her favor. I'm the only one allowed to see her anymore. Apart from her nibbles, of course." He gestured at the door and the shepherdess now long gone.

"You don't say? How fascinating. Only you? You *are* special, Mr Theris. I couldn't see her, could I? I'm almost a shepherdess." Dimity puffed up her chest and tried to look innocent and wholesome and countrified.

"Oh no, certainly not, Mrs Carefull. She's very, very particular. And what do you mean, shepherdess? That was clearly a milkmaid."

Dimity smiled again. "Oh well, perhaps someday. I do so long to meet a vampire queen. Shall we go in?"

The meal was not typical for vampires. Generally speaking, each member of a hive would sit at table with a human kneeling next to them. After the humans who were invited as guests to eat (and not *be* eaten) had begun their first course, the vampires would begin gently sipping.

Dimity had never attended such a supper party, but she had read about them.

In the Nottingham Hive, however, supper was somewhat different. As they entered the dining room, they were confronted by three seated vampires, with three empty chairs across from them. No kneeling humans at all.

Dimity wondered how all three would sip off Mr Theris at once. Would each stand, walk around the table, and take a bite, as if he were a buffet?

Clearly not. Instead, it appeared the vampires intended to simply sit on the other side of the table and stare at the three humans while they ate. It felt a little like they were specimens under observation. Dimity was grateful for her impeccable table manners.

Opposite them, Lord Finbar sat in the center. To his left was Lord Kirby. On his right was a veritable waif of a person. A frail brunette, with enormous dark eyes, a perfect heart-shaped face, and full Cupid's bow lips.

"Justice," said Lord Finbar, as if pronouncing it upon them. Had Dimity not read the file, she would never have realized it was the name of the waif.

Justice Wignall was the youngest member of the hive, only around fifty or so, and really quite lovely. Dimity had never seen a man so pretty before. Extraordinary. It was near impossible to tell if he was a man or a woman – instead, he occupied a liminal space between, like an underhill fae out of Irish folklore. Dimity only thought of him as male because the file told her to.

Justice was dressed to bridge the two as well. The only member of the hive Dimity had yet seen not wearing black, although he was still in velvet. Justice wore white – one of those soft billowing shirts commonly seen on operatic pirates. Presumably, there were britches or trousers as well, but the shirt was so dramatically oversized it was difficult to deduce more at table. It was loose about the neck so that it fell to one side, exposing one delicate white shoulder. Justice's hair was long and flowing free, and unlike the other vampires, glossy and full. He was painfully slender about the face and throat, but he didn't look hungry so much as sculpted.

Dimity swallowed down a little awe. Never had she thought to meet a man prettier than she. He also seemed, for lack of a better word, *lost*.

While Lord Kirby glowered at them and Lord Finbar slouched in gloom and (presumably) thought of poetry, Justice didn't even seem to see them, instead getting distracted by the flickering shadows cast by the candles on the tablecloth. Occasionally, he floated a hand up to rest it on the tabletop, as if his wrist were pulled up on a string. Then that hand would slowly slide off while the other rose. It was hypnotic.

The food was served all in one by Mr Theris, the plates made up with a selection of meat pies and stewed fruit, simple fare from the local bakery. Clearly, the hive no longer had even a cook. Dimity passed half of hers to Sir Crispin, as he clearly required more fuel. Once they finished, no one came to whisk their plates away, and there seemed to be no pudding course in the offing. Truly, Mr Theris was the only one left. He simply sat, looking bored.

Lord Finbar cleared his throat and began what could only be a hive meeting.

Dimity thought it very mean that they'd not been served claret with supper *or* port to follow. The hive could more than afford libations. This one pretended to be run down, but she knew from BUR's paperwork that there was money in the coffers. Vampires tended to invest well and thoughtfully, even the roves. There was no such thing as a poor vampire – not in England.

"As our guests appear seen to, we must get on with the evening's activities. Mr and Mrs Carefull, you are most welcome to our humble home, and as you aren't our drones, just yet," Finbar intoned, "you must excuse our not entertaining you after dinner, as we must hunt."

Dimity gave a little gasp. They were *hunting*, were they? Hunting the unwilling? That was strictly forbidden. They would need to report that fact to BUR immediately.

Justice – and somehow it was impossible to think of him by anything but his given name – mustered up a tiny smile. "Don't looked so shocked, darlings. Nothing so dire as actual hunting, I assure you. What he means to say is we have pubs to visit and humans to court into offering their necks. It's always consensual, I promise most faithfully."

"Speak for yourself, larva. I intend to hunt like the true vampire I am!" grumbled Lord Kirby, eyeing Dimity's neck covetously.

Lord Finbar coughed. "Speaking of, Cinjin, I need you to check our queen's chambers when she takes her bath. One of the neighbors has gone missing. I thought we'd been supplying her highness steadily, but one never knows what trauma may flow from the perpetual lament and crystal tears of our great and grieving lady, does one?"

Dimity thought this might be a joke, but couldn't be certain.

Mr Theris nodded and stood to leave. The others followed. Lord Finbar and Lord Kirby quit the room without acknowledging Dimity or Cris again. Only Justice gave them an absent smile before he drifted out.

They were left alone in the candlelight.

"Well, I say," said Dimity.

"One couldn't agree more," replied Sir Crispin, in a sepulchral parody of Lord Finbar.

At one point in his life, Sir Crispin Bontwee might have experienced an odder meal or a more peculiar set of introductions, but he was hard pressed to remember it. Lacking any further social obligations, he and Dimity made their way back to their dilapidated room.

As they walked up the stairs Dimity said loudly, no doubt in the hope that they were overheard, "Well, husband, it seems our worst fears are realized. I'm going to need more French fashion papers, that's certain. And probably an additional book of Latin verse. I'm thinking transcendentalism might be in order, too. Oh, and I'll need more paints. I'm feeling inspired by cerulean at the moment. Can you feel it? Definitely cerulean."

"Of course, my dear," said Cris, equally loudly.

Dimity was providing reasons for them to leave the

hive. Because she knew that what they must do next was contact the nearest BUR offices with their initial findings. They'd ascertained that the male vampires were *hunting* and the missing drones possibly all *dead*. On the bright side, the queen was eating full meals of milkmaids. On the down side, she might have killed a neighbor.

Dimity no doubt understood that the local BUR outpost should be alerted. If nothing else, a hive gone mad was quite a bit of paperwork. But Cris didn't think she understood that BUR was likely to order Dimity and Cris out and a sundowner in to kill the whole hive. He didn't like keeping her in the dark about it. Cris was a safety, not a secret keeper.

So in their room, before changing, he activated Dimity's auditory disruptor and pulled her close to whisper in her ear. "Did Bertie warn you of the consequence of our failing this mission?"

Dimity shook her head against him, breath quick. "No, what is it?"

"Sundowner."

Dimity gasped. "You're authorized?"

"No. You?"

"No. So they'll bring in an outsider."

Cris tried not to inhale a strand of her hair. "Lord Maccon, most likely."

Dimity gave a tiny *harrumph*. "He's reputed to be effective... but a werewolf. That's not good. He'll take out the queen? They think she's that bad?"

Crispin didn't want to tell her the whole – she had a soft heart and so far, none of the vampires they'd met deserved to die. They'd been grumpy, rude, and distracted, but that was no reason to kill a man. Mr Theris was another matter.

"No, they'll kill all four of them."

Dimity started. "The whole hive? Dead? Oh, but they don't seem so bad. Why wasn't I told?"

"Didn't want you overwrought by the timeline and the consequences, I suspect."

Dimity bristled. "I've worked under pressure before, but I suppose this is more dire than usual." She paused, almost eagerly leaning against him now, forgetting their intimate embrace in her earnestness to both communicate and be as quiet as possible. "We *must* save them."

Crispin hoped she'd say that. He'd hoped the threat would stiffen her resolve, not throw her into a panic. Of course his Sparkles was made of sterner stuff.

Indeed, her crafty mind was already working on a new approach. "I need a better plan. Even I am not a good enough seductress to save a hive from death using eyelash fluttering and late-night confessions. Besides, with the possible exception of Mr Theris, and you took him off the table, I don't think any of them are particularly interested in my wiles. We need to concentrate on extracting the queen. I should—"

"Let's talk about this later, Sparkles, at tea in town? Surely one of the teahouses in Nottingham keeps London hours."

"Tea is a lovely idea. I really need tea. We haven't been served it *once* since we arrived."

Cris enjoyed the idea of getting out of this gloomy place and escorting Sparkles to a teahouse. She would get all bright and bubbly and delighted by the improved atmosphere, and he would be seen in public with her as his wife. It wasn't real, of course, but the very idea puffed him up with pride.

Dimity frowned. "Perhaps we should not tell BUR of our initial findings? I don't want them to panic and accelerate the schedule. I need time to figure all of this out. The last thing we want is a growling sundowner in the wings."

"I agree, but the danger isn't to be discounted. They are *hunting*, Sparkles. There is a good chance the drones are dead." Cris was torn – his duty dictated that he get her out now that they knew how risky the situation, but then the hive would die. Or he could trust in his Sparkles and her abilities to fix this in two weeks. That left only him to keep her safe from possibly feral vampires. And he wasn't trained for vampires.

Dimity moved away. "This definitely calls for tea."

Budgy Hall was located close to the center of Nottingham, so fortunately they need not hire a carriage. Or worse, try to activate the hive's. They could walk. The city was modern enough to have good, strong lamplight and clean cobbles for their late-night stroll.

Dimity wore a pale peach visiting dress that made her skin appear luminous. It had some sort of shiny stripe to it, a square neckline with big buttons down the front, and a matched bonnet. Around her neck she had clasped an elaborate gold and pearl necklace. She looked pure and fresh-faced, as if butter wouldn't melt in her mouth. When occupying a role, her steps were shorter and with more sway to the hips. When she wasn't being Honey Bee, she was naturally a purposeful walker with a long stride. One of the first things Cris had ever noticed about her, after the hair, was that he didn't outpace her. And he outpaced most people.

Because they'd said they would (in a manner that had likely been overheard), they did a little shopping around Nottingham first. It was after ten, but many of the best shops were still open. Fashionable hours, indeed. Fortunate, this, as Mr and Mrs Carefull needed to be noticed and known in the town. They didn't buy much – paints (to keep up appearances) and some tea – but Cris noted the way Dimity's eyes lingered on a pair of opal drop earrings set in gold filigree.

He'd read the reports on Dimity Plumleigh-Teignmott, AKA Honey Bee. He'd read them more times than was necessary, truth be told. Listed under her susceptibilities and weaknesses were expensive jewelry, baked meringues, and handsome men. Also noted was the fact that, while *weaknesses,* no one was quite certain whether these might be exploited, as she'd encountered a great deal of all three during her service to the Crown and to date had never lost her wits over any of them. But the file said it was a possibility.

Cris thought he'd like to try all three at once. And hoped he qualified as handsome enough for the Honey Bee.

She moved with confidence around this city she'd never visited before. He fell into a back guard position without meaning to – less lead and more escort.

Without his even realizing it had happened, they were bypassing the local BUR offices and entering a teahouse.

Dimity started in with her new plan as soon as the tea arrived. Fortunately for them, the teahouse was mostly deserted. It might keep London hours, but it was clear not all that many in Nottingham did.

"I am thinking we need to lure the baroness back into society." Dimity spoke in modified code, just in case, avoiding mention of their being vampires and pretending this was more a matter of aristocratic family dynamics. She was very good.

Cris nodded for her to continue.

She nibbled a bit of apple charlotte. "I must redecorate and meddle. If I cause enough fuss and ruckus, she might get curious."

"Or territorial." He liked the idea, admittedly mostly because it didn't involve seduction.

"Hard to know for certain, since we don't know why she withdrew in the first place. I'll have to work on them for that information. But if I also make the place pretty, maybe once we get her back up, she'll want to stay."

Cris accepted a fresh cup of tea. "You'll need to take over housekeeper duties. Theris isn't going to like that. He seems to want them dependent on him."

"Yes, I noticed that, too. I'll be housekeeper if you'll be steward."

"Not butler?"

"Do you buttle then, husband?"

"Not at all well."

Her grin was full of mischief and he adored it.

"This is going to be fun, and if I can pull it off in two weeks, it's also a good one to go out on."

"Go out on, Sparkles? What do you mean?" Was she leaving the War Office? Was she leaving him? He felt a sudden sick dread. They didn't always work together, but the possibility that his next mission might be with her was one of the reasons he kept doing missions at all.

She gave him an assessing look. "That's not important. Not right now. I haven't made my final decision yet. I'm waiting on someone, you see?"

Cris had no idea what she was on about. Clearly he was losing the code to her enigmatic nature. He decided he had enough to worry about.

They returned to Budgy Hall in the small hours clutching a few small packages and feeling a renewed sense of purpose. They were asleep shortly thereafter, and Crispin even let himself enjoy her soft body curled against his.

Vampires did not bestir themselves during the day, and after years of service, no doubt Mr Theris kept entirely nighttime hours. Therefore, Dimity felt it wise to get up the next morning when they might not be interfered with. Sir Crispin agreed.

First things first.

Dimity and Sir Crispin got hot cross buns from the bakery down the way and then went 'round to the local domestics agency to retain parlormaids. Three of them. Dimity enquired after a cook, scullery maid, footmen, and butler, but was told those positions would take longer to fill. Sir Crispin did as well as he could pretending to be a new steward (really, the man was soldier-stiff sometimes and not a good actor) while she played housekeeper (with consummate aplomb) and no one even questioned their authority or their settling of Budgy Hall's account. Few knew that the Hall was a hive house. It was considered nothing more than an upstanding residence of unprecedented eccentricity and pecuniary liquidity. In other words, one did not quibble with requests from staff representing weird wealthy aristocrats. Dimity and Crispin looked to be respectable folk, exactly the kind of couple eccentric toffs would hire to manage their earthly concerns.

The agency was an efficient one and shortly after the midday toll, three fresh-faced young lasses were on the stoop.

Dimity immediately put them to work. One dusting, one sweeping and beating out carpets, and the third washing whatever needed to be washed. Which was most anything washable.

Then she took measurements and sent lovely, tolerant Sir Crispin back out to order new curtains. For the entire house.

She began to draw up lists of means by which Budgy Hall might be modernized, what needed to be stocked, who else must be hired, and what tradesmen's services should be contracted. They'd need the sweeps round to see to all the chimneys. She wanted the roof looked at because there was definitely a leak in the upstairs hallway, and of course she threw open every window sash she could, to air out the place. No one was awake to stop her. She explained to the new maids that the residents were very fashionable indeed, and did not bestir themselves until visiting hours that evening. They were to be left in their rooms upstairs, undisturbed. The girls found this entirely understandable. After all, had they been wealthy lords and ladies of leisure, they would have done the same.

Dimity nodded sagely. "Wouldn't we all, darlings? Wouldn't we all?"

She thought about getting flowers in, but then decided perhaps next week would be better, after everything was shipshape and the initial shock had worn off. Fresh flowers might be too much for vampires right away.

Presuming she had a next week. Sir Crispin had given her some leeway, but she knew that if anything concretely confirmed the drones dead or the hunting deadly, he would whisk her away and the hive would be doomed. He'd been kind to give her this chance, but he was an honest man and he took his duty as safety seriously. Too seriously.

The unusual amount of activity in the house eventually woke Mr Theris, who came down blinking in the afternoon light, and clearly annoyed by a change to his abode and schedule.

"What on earth is going on here?"

Dimity spared a moment to wish Sir Crispin were back, because the actor looked almost violent. Then she remembered that she was trained for this kind of thing, and most people were not at their best when first waking up.

"Mr Theris, there you are. I thought I would make a few minor improvements to the place while we are staying with you. I need room to paint, you see, breathing space, liberty, freedom! All this clutter and dust about, it interferes with my creative impulses. No doubt, as a noted actor yourself, you feel similarly? Speaking of which, isn't this terribly early for you? Should you not return to your chambers? I assure you, I have everything well in hand." She gave him a look that said this was perfectly normal behavior for visitors to a hive.

The man went from angry to confused. "What? Is this a dream? What is going on? Now, Mrs Carefull, I don't think you should. Not take down the curtains, Mrs Carefull, they've not been moved in a hundred years."

"All the more reason to see them cleaned."

"Absolutely not!"

"You're quite right. Why bother cleaning them? We should replace them entirely. What a good idea, Mr Theris. Blue, do you think?"

He sputtered at her, now part anger and part confusion, still bleary-eyed.

Dimity gave him her best, most winsome smile. "No, you're correct. Not blue. Something lighter. Cream, perhaps? Or pale pink?" Dimity tapped her cheek with the feathered quill (it was the only writing implement she'd been able to find, and frankly, she was startled the ink pot hadn't dried out). She added wallpaper stripping and whitewashing to her list and then wondered about reupholstering the sitting room, at the very least. Surely it had to be done?

"Mrs Carefull, stop distracting me. What *is* this chaos?" He gestured at the three neat maids who were working diligently in an entirely *not* chaotic manner.

"Chaos, oh, you are droll. It's simply a bit of light cleaning. Go back to bed, do. Think of how nice and sweet-smelling everything will be when you rouse again."

He looked like he might remove her bodily from the house, and then eject the new maids, except that Sir Crispin returned at that juncture and gave him a threatening glare. Clearly too tired to deal with surprise cleaning sessions from invading artists, the drone threw up his hands. "I can't cope with this right now! I'll speak to you both later, after dark, and we'll see what Lord Finbar makes of these presumptuous ways of yours."

"I hardly think cleaning is *tricky*, Mr Theris. Sensible, more like," replied Dimity, knowing she shouldn't press, but Sir Crispin was there making her feel quite safe, as was his wont, and she did so love having the last word.

Mr Theris glared at them both and then retreated back upstairs.

"That went well," said Sir Crispin, putting down his packages.

"He definitely thinks this is his domain."

"He might be quite violent in its defence. A man like that, with a small amount of power. He'll guard it jealously."

Dimity nodded, "I agree, but you forget I can defend myself."

"You would show our hand if you did. What would a busybody artist know of such things?"

"Fair point. Now, about those curtains?"

With only three maids, she could only get so much done, and Dimity kept having to send Sir Crispin – Cris – out after something or another. He seemed willing. After all, he liked to be given tasks. He liked to be in motion, and Dimity was beginning to suspect, for all his frowns and grumping at her, that he liked pleasing her, too.

Nevertheless, by the time the sun set and the vampires were scheduled to rise from the dead, Dimity felt that they'd made an excellent start.

Lord Finbar came down first. He blinked, made a snuffling noise that might have been approval when he noticed a maid and her duster. He even, perhaps, understood on some level that things downstairs had all been cleaned. Of course, he muttered something about how dusters intruded on the sanctity of his enduring loneliness.

"Now, Lord Finbar," Dimity made herself known to the vampire, bustling up to him and taking his arm in a comforting manner, "you leave the nice girl to her duties. She's doing an excellent job. Come along with me and see what I've discovered in the library. That painting I wrote to you about, the one I found the record of the baroness buying? Well, it is indeed here in your collection. It's hanging in the library and it's so very beautiful! I know my friend coordinating the Dutch masters exhibition in London would simply love to borrow it."

Lord Finbar was clearly befuddled, but he was passive enough under her influence.

Dimity wondered if he had even noticed the staff

had gone in the first place, and whether the reappearance of parlormaids felt more to him as if they had never been gone.

"But could they not dust during the daylight hours?" he complained.

Dimity patted his velvet-covered arm. "It's only just after sunset. And while I'm sure they could, there's a bit of extra tidying to do, this once. Could you not be patient, for me?" She made her eyes big and looked longingly up into his long, somber face.

"But what about the depths of my ennui? Have you considered that, my dear Mrs Carefull? No, you have not. Why? Because everyone always forgets about *me and my woes*."

Dimity guided him towards the library, one of the first rooms she'd had cleaned, exactly for this reason – because she'd guessed it was Lord Finbar's territory and she wanted it ready when he came down. Lord Finbar seemed like the kind of man, vampire or not, who liked a library above all else. "I'm here for you now, *dear* Lord Finbar. And I was thinking of you and your melancholy when I realized that a few teeny-weeny, oh-so-minor changes would improve matters for you no end. Just think, no dust means no sneezing. Nothing disturbs a good despondency like a sneeze. Don't you agree? So, this will help you with that. I'm so charmed by your wonderful house, but don't you think it a *touch* gloomy? Just brightening it up a mite will mean your own natural moroseness will be more striking by contrast. When you're feeling better, we'll discuss replacing the throw rugs. They're doing wonderful things with *color* these days, you know? I was thinking something restful for the sitting room. What's that color of the sky midafternoon?"

"Blue?" suggested Lord Finbar, looking lost.

"Yes, but what's it named?"

"Sky blue?"

"Yes, that's the stuff. Or robin's egg. So lovely in the spring, don't you feel? Although of course you don't have the opportunity see a blue sky, do you? Well never you mind about that. I'll simply do over the whole sitting room to remind you of how lovely the spring is."

"In blue?"

"Exactly, as you say, blue. What an excellent suggestion, Lord Finbar. You're brilliant! Blue is exactly the thing for the sitting room. Why didn't I think of it?"

"I am? You didn't?"

Dimity nodded reassuringly, and guided him into the library at last. "We will design it to remind you of all the possibilities in life and daylight. It will inspire considerable verse, I promise. Now, about this painting..."

She'd left Lord Finbar staring at an oil of an unfortunately chubby horse, cheeky goat, and three chickens that had hung in the library for two hundred years as though he had never seen it before.

When Lord Kirby emerged, on the other hand, he said nothing. Dimity was thinking about how to balance her new housekeeper duties with her front as an artist, and was considering getting out her paints or sketching a bit while the maids worked.

Lord Kirby ran his hand down the newly waxed

stair railing as he mooched downstairs.

"Did you know there was mahogany under all that dust, Lord Kirby?"

"I did, Mrs Carefull." He spoke at last, in a low, sharp voice, but clear, with bite to it. A pudgy man like that ought not to be birdlike, but Dimity found him so. His eye movements were almost too quick, unnaturally so. His steps too, especially when compared to Lord Finbar's oozing slouch.

As he ran his fingers down the banister, the long sleeve of his robe trailed becomingly. Dimity would have said something complimentary to that effect, but she wasn't certain yet what her tactics should be with this vampire.

"Lord Finbar is in the library," she informed him.

"Lord Finbar is always in the library," grumbled Lord Kirby, darting down the hall presumably towards one of the other rooms. He barely glanced at the new maids – if anything, he seemed shy of them.

Sir Crispin returned shortly after that, to find Dimity rearranging the sitting room to better aesthetic effect. This had started because she wanted to use a writing desk there on which to paint.

"You're a menace, you are," he said, fondly. He had packages under one arm and more beeswax in hand.

Dimity put her hands on her hips and grinned at him. "This is *so much fun*." Rearranging furniture was leagues better than seducing people.

"Bed anytime soon?" he asked.

Dimity thought he sounded hopeful, or she hoped he sounded hopeful. By rights they should be trying to stay awake, to learn more about the hive and adjust to entirely night-time hours, but they'd had a very long day already.

Justice came flitting downstairs then. He cast himself dramatically over the railing at the top and then sort of a wafted down like a leaf waving back and forth, side to side, in the breeze.

Lord Kirby re-emerged form wherever he'd gone and said in his cutting voice, "You saw *that human* again last night, didn't you, Justice? He'll break your heart into a thousand pieces, he will."

Dimity stared at Lord Kirby in amazement. Who knew the man was capable of such emotion? True, it seemed to be exasperated contempt, and he was reprimanding a fellow vampire of at least fifty years old as though he were his father. But at least Lord Kirby was reacting to something.

Justice, waifish and frail, paused in mid-descent and pressed a hand to his perfect forehead. "Oh, but I love him so ardently. How can I resist such a man as Gantry Ogdon-Loppes? I ask you?" He spread his delicate fingers wide and cast them over Dimity, Cris, and Lord Kirby below, as if in benediction. The single gas sconce on the wall behind him cast a nimbus of pale light about his thick curls. He pouted fiercely.

Lord Kirby persisted. "You're a vampire. He's a human. It'll never work."

"Oh, I know it won't work! But what magic we shall wring from out our hearts with the trying of it – until we both fail tragically and all is in ruins!"

With which he whirled about and drifted back up the stairs, apparently having decided he was not yet ready to face the world. He had not noticed the cleaning at all. Clearly, he had other concerns.

Dimity made certain the maids were out of hearing and well occupied before she turned curiously to Lord Kirby. "Why not turn the lucky fellow into a drone?"

Lord Kirby only held up a hand and walked away.

Dimity looked to Cris. A glimmer of hope! "My darling husband, embrace me."

Sir Crispin rolled his eyes and did so, allowing her to stand on tippy-toe in order to whisper as quietly as might be, directly in his ear. "If Justice's *amore* is a younger son of a progressive family, offering him a drone position should be a very tempting prospect."

"Unless he's married, of course," Sir Crispin whispered (sensibly) back.

Dimity could not help but be a little shocked. "Do you think that likely?"

Cris leaned back and glowered at her, clearly not caring if this bit were overheard by the sensitive ears of a vampire or a parlormaid. "We are dealing with the country gentry, Sparkles. Anything scandalous is possible. Now, I'm for bed, before you send me on another errand."

Dimity watched him climb the stairs. It must be admitted she did this with a great deal of enjoyment. Sir Crispin did have very fine legs.

CHAPTER FIVE

In Which Sir Crispin Critiques Tennyson

Cris had another restless sleep due to torturous cuddles from Sparkles. They still had no fire in their room, as the chimney had yet to be cleaned, so it was quite frigid. He couldn't very well deny her his warmth, now, could he? He arranged himself innocently in bed well before her. She climbed in with a great deal more alacrity than previously, and curled up against him without flinching at all.

He adored it, of course. Therein lay the problem.

Apparently, she was already accustomed to him in her bed. A truly dangerous situation because *accustomed* would lead to *expectation* and that edged into *need*, a potent aphrodisiac indeed. Cris knew himself well enough to understand how much he enjoyed being needed. Even if it was only for warmth.

He thought she might be sniffing him, for as she nuzzled up against his shoulder, puffs of breath ghosted over his skin.

"I think things are coming along very well, don't you?" she whispered. His skin pricked under the sensation of her words.

"Clean curtains might have been enough. You seem intent on miracles."

"Pish-tosh, this place needs brightening and organization if we're to lure the queen above ground. The supernatural is all very well and good, but it mustn't be allowed to get untidy. What we have here is a veritable horror."

"Why do you think they call it *going to Goth*?"

"Well, I intend to put a stop to it."

"Might not work – we still don't know what drove away the queen."

"Give me time."

"I don't want you going to confront her alone, Sparkles. Too dangerous."

"I can take care of myself, thank you very much."

"I'm your safety, remember? Allow me some use beyond fetching and carrying beeswax."

"If you insist." She inhaled him again, a little more obviously this time. Dimity never did anything obviously without intent, so he took that as permission to relax into his own inclinations.

He allowed himself the luxury of bending his head to bury his nose in the crown of her sweet-smelling hair. He hadn't helped brush it tonight and she had it plaited back for sleep. A great loss. "Why, for goodness sake, must you smell like lemon and honey? And is that milk as well?"

"Mmm." She was falling asleep, comforted by his annoyance. It was familiar ground.

"It's ridiculous that you look the way you do and also smell heavenly."

"I wash my hair in a lemon rinse twice a week,

when I can get the fruit. And then bicarbonate of soda, to keep it soft afterwards. I'm terribly vain, you see. The lemon keeps my color bright. I could go out in the sun, of course, but that would ruin my complexion. Which is why I use milk and honey on my face most nights." Her voice was muffled in his nightshirt. She yawned and her jaw creaked. "I wash it off with cold water after. You should try it sometime. Leaves the skin nice and soft. Not that you—" She yawned again. "— should necessarily muck about with your face at all. It's lovely the way it is."

And she drifted off.

He lay, still as he could, once again trying desperately not to scare her off with the depths of his wanting. Although, since she had openly admitted to thinking his face lovely, perhaps the wanting was mutual?

He found himself wondering how her milk-scented skin would look against the roughened darkness of his. He lifted his hand, the one that she wasn't leaning against, and covered her small one where it rested on his chest. He entwined their fingers, lightly.

So far as the cleaning and redecorating was concerned, Dimity was having a wonderful time. The hive house was beginning to smell less musty. Sir Crispin, while eager to assist with cleaning and curtains, was proving difficult as a prospective husband. Dimity had decided to seduce him, but she had less than a fortnight in which to do it. It seemed to her quite easy to fix an entire hive, spruce it up, make it happy again, in the space of two weeks, but seducing Sir Crispin? That looked likely to be the work of months. He was awfully resistant to her charms. Last night she'd draped herself over him, and nuzzled.

Nothing.

Nuzzled, mind you. What was a girl to do when a light nuzzling didn't encourage at least a kiss on the cheek? He'd nuzzled back, but only the top of her head. It wasn't like that was a significant location. At least, her seduction lessons hadn't said so. She wished suddenly for her dear friend Sophronia, who had herself a lover of many years, and could explain the significance of a reciprocal nuzzle. Unfortunately, Sophronia was most likely off killing a tyrannical mastermind, or overthrowing a secret society, or stopping a pudding war, or some other such nonsense of deep political importance.

No one would ever accuse Dimity of being ambitious. In fact, her stated goal in life had never been espionage, even though both her parents were evil geniuses. She came by her skills naturally and honed them with training, so she ended up in a devious career despite herself. But she had always wanted to do something she really loved, one day. And that one day had come, and that something was Sir Crispin.

He was proving impossibly stoic, always had done. She suspected that was why she'd come to adore him. But her usual tactics of flirtation were not effective on a man who worked alongside professional flirts, and thus saw wiles applied on the regular. He was disposed to find her disingenuous. Which was not unfair. It was only that Dimity had been at the game so long, she wasn't sure she remembered how to actually be *genuine*.

With her friends, perhaps. Sophronia and Sidheag when they had an opportunity to gather, or Agatha when she was in town. With them she could be herself. With them she even confessed to her secret desires – a house in the country, a husband, children. They thought her frivolous, but at least they did not mock. But seeing her true friends was rare enough an occurrence that Dimity wondered if she was losing track of herself. If she'd become, over the years, nothing more than the Honey Bee – effective, shining, and shallow.

It was a pickle. For if her wiles *did* work on Sir Crispin, she would not trust him so much. For he then would have been taken in by the Honey Bee, not Dimity. And she would never know if he really liked her. But her wiles were all she knew of relating to a man. How was she to seduce him without them?

So now, they had this awkward dance, where she carefully let down her guard and did *not* flirt at all. And he'd brushed her hair as if he treasured the task, and curved his arm about her after he thought she'd fallen asleep. She found herself thinking when she awoke still cuddled against him, his fingers tentatively laced with hers, and the afternoon sun making pink of her eyelids, that this was the *good bit*. That this might be all she really wanted. Just him, and a sun she rarely saw, and something warm coiling between them.

But he was so careful to get out of bed without waking her, as if afraid of what she might do and how he might react. As if afraid of her. Which hurt a bit. So she kept her eyes shut until she heard him leave the room to head out to the local bakery and fetch them a meal.

Dimity dressed in moss green, a favorite older dress suited to an artist, with a fern pattern and a charming little matched belt. Since it had a relatively high collar and a complex pattern, she went with bold drop earrings, massive square emeralds. Paste, of course – all of Dimity's jewelry was paste. Real wasn't the point as far as she was concerned. With the Honey Bee in action, real was *never* the point. Sometimes, in fact, the point was the *point* – her jewelry could get very sharp.

As she descended the stairs in the early afternoon she knew she made a picture, a fresh brightness in the rundown gloom of Budgy Hall. She found Sir Crispin dealing with a crowd of tradesfolk at the hive house door. The mess of activity in the entranceway paused to watch her graceful arrival.

Sir Crispin said proudly, "My wife, Mrs Carefull. She's really in charge, of course. How are you today, my lovely general?"

"Topping, darling husband. Good afternoon, everyone, have you all learned your duties?"

A chorus of agreement and nods met her question. There were chimney sweeps, and paper strippers, white washers, laundresses, and seamstresses in abundance.

Dimity gave them her very best smile. Most of the

gentlemen and one of the ladies sighed in admiration. She memorized their faces, of course.

"I shall be in the sitting room, painting, if you need to consult me on anything. Please do not hesitate to interrupt. Like most artists, I dearly love an interruption. As my husband has no doubt told you, the other residents of the house are of the fashionable set. They keep London hours, and are not to be disturbed. When they do deign to come downstairs, please don't take anything they say to heart. Just come find me if something wants sorting." She was not worried that they might realize the residents were vampires – after all, anyone who was anyone kept London hours. It wouldn't do to be out before sunset – one might get *tan*.

Tradespeople, of course, understood the eccentricities of the upper classes. More nods met her remarks.

Dimity smiled at them, pleased. "Very well, then, to work with us all."

She turned to find the three parlormaids waiting patiently in the drawing room. She wondered how long they had been there and immediately put them on an afternoon rotation forthwith – instructing them to arrive midday and stay until just after supper. Unlike the tradesfolk, who were temporary, staff needed to become slowly accustomed to the members of the hive. Smart staff under regular exposure would eventually realize that they were surrounded by vampires, but hopefully by then a certain amount of loyalty and tolerance would have built up. They might even become interested in increasing their income with drone status. The three girls seemed bright, eager, and sensible – excellent candidates, in Dimity's limited experience.

She set them to cleaning and preparing the kitchen and back rooms, in the hopes that more staff might be forthcoming. Then she arranged her easel in the sitting room so that it was visible from the hallway, and began to paint.

Cris ran several more errands for Dimity in his guise as longsuffering husband, retrieved an extensive spread to feed the masses come suppertime, and returned home a good hour before sunset. He found the house humming with useful activity and Dimity in full artist persona artistically flourishing a brush at what appeared to be a bilious interpretation of a frolicking cow. He hid a broad grin – her artistic skills were indeed rather poor – and asked the parlormaids to arrange the food in the dining room.

Then, screwing his courage to the sticking point, he went up to their room and donned his dancing attire. This took every ounce of willpower he had. The outfit had been provided to him, with great amusement, by Bertie. The impossible fellow seemed to feel that a man who did ballet must perforce wear a combination of bathing costume and strong man circus attire. It was blue and white striped and indecently tight.

But he and Sparkles must make an artistic impression on the vampires, and if that required stripes, Sir Crispin would do his duty to his country and wear stripes.

He returned downstairs, wearing a dressing robe over said stripes, to find that Sparkles had left the cow to dry, and was dabbing at a smaller sheet featuring an insipid landscape, perhaps Devonshire, with a huge portly floating insect of some kind in the gray sky.

"Is that a caterpillar?" Cris inquired, curious.

Dimity tilted her head. "No, a dirigible. Or it will be in a bit."

"Looks like a caterpillar."

Dimity smiled at him. "I know. I'm really very bad."

"I like your frolicking cow."

"Dog! Please."

"Oh, is it?"

"Clearly *that* is a hound on the hunt. It's my commentary on the false joy of the class system, which is, in fact, nested in repression of the working folk and compounded by the everyman search for meaning in this cold, desolate world."

"Oh," said Crispin.

"I shall title it, of course, The Frolicking Cow. What are you wearing, husband?"

"My robe, of course. I'm going to practice."

She twinkled at him. "Of course you are. I shall return to my floating caterpillar, shall I?"

"By all means. It's nearly sunset. We must put on a good show."

"Frolicking cows notwithstanding."

He left her to it. First, he opened up the huge double doors between the sitting room, where she sat painting, and the drawing room, which was a larger space, less cluttered now the maids had finished with it. Then, he pushed back the furniture, but this did not give him nearly enough space. Fortunately, the reupholsterer arrived and took most of the chairs and couches away. That helped considerably.

The rugs were removed by some dustmen. Dimity said she'd simply gone ahead and ordered all new ones from London, which left Cris with a nice wide bare floor. It was dusty, even after the parlormaids swept it, and warped by age and ill maintenance. Also, it boasted rather too many dark stains for his liking, because they made him think of vampires and blood, but it was good enough to be going on with.

He threw off his robe to giggles from one of the maids and a tiny gasp from Dimity. He glared at the maid, who scuttled away quickly, making him feel like a shabby gentleman. When he turned to Dimity she was back at her painting, a little color in her cheeks. Probably embarrassed by his poor manners.

"I'm going to stretch now, wife," he warned her.

"Are you indeed, husband?" she responded, oddly breathless. "Are you certain that outfit will accommodate such a trial? It's rather tight."

"Apparently it's made for just such an endeavor."

"Praise be to the heavens," murmured Dimity.

Crispin took that as sarcasm. "I shall now be the frolicking cow."

Dimity looked him over, hazel eyes eager and shy. "My dear husband, there is nothing at all bovine about you. Please do carry on." He would have thought this a trained manoeuvre except she was also crimson faced. Clearly she wanted to stare at certain parts of his anatomy. His Sparkles was demonstrating equal parts embarrassment and arousal.

She licked her lips, unconsciously, he was certain. "Frolic away, darling, do." Her voice had gone a little hoarse.

Cris concentrated hard on the absurdity of his striped costume in order to suppress his body's natural response to her desire while simultaneously blessing the tan complexion that hid his own fierce blush. Then he turned away and focused on putting on a good showing.

Cris remembered some of his old stretches, and he combined those with the ones he used before fencing. He admitted to losing himself a bit in the moment, even without music, even knowing she was casting little glances his way. Thus, he didn't really notice when the sun set and the gas came on.

When he surfaced from a series of deep lunges, most of the day laborers seemed to have departed, but a good many of the more dedicated tradesfolk remained. He was ashamed that he'd lost track of time so thoroughly.

Dimity rose and stretched herself, or as much as she might in stays and tight sleeves. She now had a small arrangement of paintings strewn about to dry and an artfully applied smudge of blue paint on her chin. She also seemed to have her blushes under control, although her gaze on him now was almost possessive.

"Shall I play for you?" She pointed to the Broadwood upright piano in the corner.

"You play?"

"Not very well and only about six things. And I'm sure that's out of tune. But they'll be awake soon and coming down. It'd be good for them to find us occupied in boldly artistic pursuits."

"If you insist," he said, feeling ever more embarrassed.

She sat and plonked out a small light piece of Austrian extraction, and he did a few experimental spins and a leap or two. He swept his hands about, remembering to curve his arms, and generally tried to behave like a complete idiot.

When the piece ended, sarcastic clapping met his final pose.

Cinjin Theris, the actor drone chappy, leaned against the doorjamb and glared at him. "You're better than I thought you'd be. Why come up to Nottingham at all, when you could clearly take the stage in London?"

"Is that what *you* desire, Mr Theris – a London debut?" Dimity rose to intercept the drone.

Cris pretended to be very concerned about the line of his foot, and did a set of point and flex in all five positions while listening intently.

"Doesn't every actor? Or dancer, for that matter."

Dimity tittered at him. "My husband is talented, my dear sir, but sadly lacks ambition."

"How very wearing that must be."

She took his arm gently and led him from the room, chatting amiably. Cris began moving what little furniture was left back into some semblance of order. Doing a little twist here and a leg lift there, making a performance out of it.

"Oh!" said a breathy voice from the hallway. "Look at you! I do so adore muscular men."

Cris paused to smile at the vampire. "Have you one of your own?"

Justice floated into the room. "My dear Gantry, the light of my life, has just such a form, so powerful. I can see now that you really are a dancer. I was one myself, did you know? Before I took the bite, of course. Ah, *before...*" He floated one arm up into the air. "Still graceful, although that's my vampire nature now, not my once plentiful creative talent. And it is so hard to force myself to move slowly, languidly, when my nature is quick and deadly. I can dance, of course, but only the learned steps, nothing inspired or original. So sad. A great loss to the adoring public, I'm sure."

Then he whirled and drifted away.

Cris stared at his retreating back with the sensation of exasperation he was beginning to associate with most vampires, and then he started and stared even harder.

Is that—? Is he wearing Dimity's *muslin nightgown?*

Cris trotted after the vampire into the entranceway and watched as Justice opened the door and drifted out into the night. That was definitely Dimity's peignoir billowing around him, swamping his small frame and trailing dramatically on the cobblestones of the street.

The vampire left the front door wide open behind him.

After a brief moment's consideration, because he was still in what amounted to a swimming costume,

Cris threw on his greatcoat, buttoned it closed, pulled on his boots, and dashed after the nightgown-clad vampire, out into the city.

Dimity would understand. Or at least, he hoped she would. Plus, she would no doubt want her nightgown back in one piece.

Dimity distracted Mr Theris with chatter for a while, then said she had to put away her paints and returned to discover that Sir Crispin had gone off somewhere, presumably following some important mission-related clue or other. Dimity hoped he'd managed to change his outfit or he would cut quite the spectacle, waltzing about in striped sportswear like a chump – nice legs notwithstanding. Not to mention his other manifold *endowments*.

She couldn't give his endowments too much thought, however, because she encountered and then became busy arguing with Lord Finbar. The vampire seemed to take great personal offense to the fact that while he'd been asleep, she'd commenced a redecoration of his entire house. Silly fellow. It would be so much *better*.

"I left your private rooms alone, didn't I?" Dimity smiled at him.

He glowered. "I asked you explicitly not to intrude upon my vast melancholy."

"How is this an intrusion? A little light dusting. The wallpaper needed to go anyway. It's only very minor things."

"But my *melancholy*."

"There were cobwebs, Lord Finbar. Cobwebs. Which, I'm bound to say, are not at all melancholic, rather, more unsanitary." She paused, but he had nothing to say to that. "Good. Now, have you met the new parlormaid, Rosie? Rosie, this is the lord and master of this domicile, Lord Finbar."

"Good evening, m'lord."

Rosie had proved herself to be, on very short acquaintance, a hardworking and practical young lady who knew which side her bread was buttered on. She would, without question, take to the fang if pecuniary advancement and steak-and-kidney pie lay at the other end of those points. Some might consider it a bit too soon to open up about the hive, but Lord Finbar clearly needed some level of practical adoration and Rosie was rather eager to please. She'd make an excellent drone, even if she wasn't in it for the immortality. The best drones often weren't, or so Dimity had heard.

Thus Dimity felt perfectly solid in saying, "You're a good girl, Rosie, and I think you'll do very well with Lord Finbar here. He's a vampire, you know?"

Rosie evaluated the oily hair and drooping velvet jacket with thoughtful brown eyes. "A real live vampire, ma'am? I'm honored."

Lord Finbar mooched in a fallen angel kind of way.

"Best we keep that between us," said Dimity.

Rosie nodded, eyes big. They softened at the sight of Lord Finbar. "I won't say nothing to no one, promise."

He glowered at her hopefully.

Dimity leaned forwards conspiratorially, implying that this next bit of information was even more exciting. "He is also a noted poet."

"Oh, my stars! A real poet? Never thought to meet one of those in my lifetime." She smiled at Lord Finbar, who looked a little pleased, but still droopy.

To Dimity, Rosie said, "Your vampire wants looking after, methinks."

Dimity winked at the girl. "I knew I could rely on your discretion. You're topping, Rosie dear. Now, Lord Finbar, don't frown so. Rosie will be working in the study this evening, giving everything there a good clean. You know what she'd like more than anything, I believe?"

Lord Finbar glowered at her. "What would *she* like, then?"

"For you to read her some Byron. Have you ever heard of Byron, Rosie?"

"No, ma'am."

"Well, there then, you see? You're exactly the right age for Byron. He had me all aflutter at your age. And if Lord Finbar reads very well and you like him enough, perhaps a snack for the nice, sad vampire. But only if you really don't mind."

Dimity whirled on Lord Finbar and made her tone fierce. "Only if she *really* doesn't mind, Lord Finbar."

Lord Finbar looked both aghast and almost excited. "Of course! What do you take me for?"

Since it was patently obvious he was a vampire and would prefer it believed that he was not to be trusted with anyone as nice as Rosie, Dimity only shook her head at him. "Behave, Lord Finbar. Perhaps do not burden Rosie with your original works, not right away. They might be too tempting for such an innocent lass. Definitely start with Byron. Speaking of which, did you know my brother is one of the leading translators of Catullus? Have you ever read Catullus, Lord Finbar? I think you might enjoy him. And I'm sure Rosie would."

But the vampire and the parlormaid had drifted away together, towards the study.

Dimity looked up to find Lord Kirby glowering at her from behind a curtain of silver hair. "What are you up to, Mrs Carefull?"

"Oh Lord Kirby, there you are! How delightful. I've precisely the thing for you to help me with."

"Help? Help!"

Something caught her eye. "Oh, pardon me just one moment."

Dimity trotted into the drawing room. "Mr Theris! You leave Miss Shortface alone! She has work to do. No, not Mr Headicar either! Really, Mr Theris, don't you have acting to do? Go learn some lines and stop seducing the tradesfolk. Honestly. They've actual responsibilities. These walls aren't going to repaper themselves."

Mr Theris shoved his wandering hands back into his trouser pockets and left the room. Horrible man.

Dimity sniffed. She supposed she was going to have to get rid of him somehow. Except that would leave the hive with no drones at all. Something to think on. "Now, Lord Kirby, where were we? Oh yes, I wonder if I might ask your advice on a matter of grave importance?"

"My advice?" The portly vampire twiddled with the tassel at the end of one long sleeve nervously. He withdrew his face a little farther behind his long hair.

There was a knock at the front door, loud enough to be heard over the general bustle, but Dimity would not be distracted again. Besides, doors were Theris's job, whether the drone liked it or not.

"Where is your husband, Mrs Carefull?" Lord Kirby asked, pointedly.

"Oh, he's somewhere."

One of the seamstresses answered the door. A young milkmaid type stood there, looking nervous.

Lord Kirby was shocked. "Oh! Finbar forgot. How could he? It's *her* suppertime." Lord Kirby cried out for all to hear. "Cinjin! She needs you, now!"

Mr Theris reemerged and gave a mocking bow to the milkmaid. "Of course. But if I could simply–"

"*Now*, Cinjin." The vampire's sleeve tassels quivered in agitation.

"Yes, sir." The actor escorted the young woman towards the back of the house and, presumably, through the kitchen to the mysterious cave where the hive queen languished.

Dimity tried to follow.

Lord Kirby grabbed her by the arm, his movement so fast as to be imperceptible to the human eye. Fortunately, no one around them noticed. Too busy. "I think *not*, Mrs Carefull. What are you after?"

Dimity ignored him, calling, "Oh Mr Theris, just one moment, please?"

She shook free of the vampire, who let her go or she wouldn't have been able, and rushed to the piano in the drawing room where she'd left one of her Parisian fashion papers. She'd needed it to explain the exact color she wanted for the new curtains, because the seamstress seemed to believe there was no difference between sage and light olive. *Heaven forfend!*

"Here you go, dear." She handed it to the milkmaid.

"What's this, ma'am?"

"Some light fashion-forward reading for the grand lady, when you're in there. I think she might be interested."

Lord Kirby tried to intervene. "Now, wait just a moment there, Mrs Carefull!"

It was Mr Theris who came to Dimity's defense. "Really, Kirby, what can it hurt?"

Lord Kirby muttered something dark about ballgowns being at the root of all evil (which made Dimity wonder) but he let the two humans continue into the depths of the hive unmolested – the baroness's meal now clutching a French fashion paper to her breast.

Dimity was pleased. "Now, Lord Kirby, about that advice I needed from you? This way, please. It's this desk, you see, the lacquer. I'm not certain it's quite salvageable..."

With some gentle encouragement, grumpy Lord Kirby was surprisingly eager to be of use in making decisions about furniture and upholstery and the like. As Dimity had surmised, he wished to be necessary and have purpose within the hive. His general anger at the world rested in Lord Finbar's neglect of his duties as praetoriani. Lord Kirby thought he could do a better job. Dimity tended to agree, but praetoriani or not, she could capitalize upon his interest.

At first, he resented her distracting him with a lacquered escritoire, and accused her of trying to ingratiate herself. Apparently, he thought she was attempting to climb the social hierarchy of the hive when she was still new and only a candidate. Although he didn't outright say any of that. But Dimity carved away at his defences throughout the course of the evening. By midnight he'd come around to her idea that making the hive house beautiful might encourage the queen to return to it, and the lack of staff (and drones) was a concern.

"Theris ran them off," he confessed. "Said some of them were lazy and found others stealing and the like. Finbar didn't care. Then before we knew it, Theris was the only one left."

"You gave them marching orders, nothing more severe?" Dimity waited with bated breath.

"We are not monsters! Even with our baroness below ground." The vampire clearly wanted to say *queen*, not *baroness*, but there were workers about. But they understood each other. Lord Kirby, at least, hadn't killed anyone. Dimity doubted Justice or Finbar had either. None of them seemed interested enough, let alone motivated enough, to deal out death. Too much effort.

"I'm very glad to hear it. You must miss them all." Her voice was mellow and sympathetic.

He looked suddenly far more sad than grumpy. "Yes, yes, I think I do. But I miss her most of all.

Although, of course, I understand her distress."

"What caused her to, you know, fade away?"

Lord Kirby bristled. "I would never speak about such shame as darkened this house. It is enough for me to know that it was not my fault! None of their leaving was my fault."

Dimity believed him too. There was no artifice in Lord Kirby. If any of the former drones or staff had been killed, she suspected he would admit to it openly. If only because he still wasn't sure about her and her husband, and would no doubt take any excuse to scare them off, or even simply scare them.

This supposition was supported when a large, fierce older woman appeared at the door and announced that she was the cook who'd left six months ago, and if that Theris chap could be made to hold his tongue and keep his hands away from the maids, she wanted her job back, thank you very much. Apparently, she'd heard Budgy Hall was hiring, and had come to see if things had been fixed to her liking.

"You know who you work for here?"

"I do, and I don't mind pointy bits so long as it's not me. Pay is good and the work hours suit me and my family, so long as I can take on my former contract."

Dimity nodded eagerly. "I'm sure we can come to some arrangement."

"You the new housekeeper?" The woman bustled in, already reaching into her sack and pulling out a pinafore.

"Only temporarily. I'm Mrs Carefull, painter. Candidate for, well, you know."

"Ah yes, I see. Well, I do like what you're doing with the place. You and yours have had supper already, I take it? How's tea in an hour or so suit you?"

"Can you serve for all those currently working?"

"Certainly, if I can borrow one of the upstairs maids."

"Please do, Mrs…?"

"Mrs Fwopwin. But Cook'll do. My sister's boy will come on for cook's assistant and I've another nephew who might do for the boot boy, if you're looking?"

Dimity gave the bossy woman an assessing look. "I'll leave everything below stairs in your clearly capable hands, Cook, shall I?"

"You and I, Mrs Carefull, are going to get along fine." Mrs Fwopwin gave her a wide, slightly mean smile and made her way towards the kitchen. "She's still hiding out in the caves, is she?"

"Yes, she is."

"You going to fix that too, Mrs Carefull?" But Cook didn't seem to want an answer to that, for she closed the staff door firmly behind her. Dimity knew the type. She was retaking possession of her domain.

Accordingly, about an hour after midnight, Dimity broke her entire team for tea. Sir Crispin still had not returned and she was growing concerned. But tea took priority.

Theris reappeared from his duty to the hive queen without the milkmaid (which gave Dimity another missing person to worry about) and surveyed the spread with shock. There were warm fresh buns and jellied eel from the local bakery, but only a proper cook could have produced fresh apple fritters and custard. Simple, wholesome fare that would buck them up for the rest of the night's work.

"Cook is back," explained Dimity.

Mr Theris flushed. "But I..."

Dimity gave him her most innocent look. "You did what, Mr Theris? Cook seems very capable. I don't know why she had to take such an extensive leave. Sick family member, I suppose. I'm sure we are all delighted to have her back. Don't you miss freshly cooked meals? I'm sure Mr Carefull and I will be pleased to have her, and it takes the burden off you. Surely an actor such as yourself shouldn't have to worry about providing and serving at table?"

"Well, yes, but—"

"See, I understand you feel a great responsibility. But you can relax now, let us take on some of the burden."

"Now wait a moment, you haven't even been officially accepted into the household. The baroness has to do that. You're very high-handed, aren't you, Mrs Carefull?"

"Am I, Mr Theris? You think me officious? I only want what's best. And prettiest. Surely a man of your discerning tastes could not abide such a house as this one was prior to my arrival? I'm sure no one meant to let it get so bad." She patted his arm, letting her hand linger. His expression mixed confusion and anger. "Oh look, here comes Lord Finbar. Do excuse me."

He stopped her with an iron grip on her arm. "I am still the only one she trusts. The only one she'll see. My place here is assured. I'm necessary. The only one left who is. You can't get rid of me and you can't replace me."

"Really, Mr Theris! Have I got rid of anyone? No. I have, in fact, done nothing but bring people in. Give me some credit for good intentions."

"Oh, you're certainly good at something, Mrs Carefull. I simply haven't figured out exactly what that is yet."

"Painting," replied Dimity, pertly. Then she twisted and dropped the weight in her shoulder, in a practiced move they'd drilled into her at Finishing School. It broke her free of his grip, although she'd have a bruise from it later.

"You should go retrieve the milkmaid, Mr Theris. Don't you think she's been below long enough?"

"Don't presume to tell me my duties, Mrs Carefull!" he hissed. But he marched towards the kitchen to, presumably, do exactly that.

Lord Finbar had trailed in after the vivacious Rosie, looking stunned but eager. Dimity went over to them, mostly to check on Rosie. The parlormaid seemed pleased as punch, with no marks to her neck as yet. But from the solicitous way in which Lord Finbar saw her seated and her plate filled, it wouldn't be too long.

Lord Kirby, in almost animated discussion with one of the carpenters on the subject of dovetail joints, looked positively chipper. Although neither one could partake of tea as yet, they both cautiously enjoyed the dining experience – in their way. They watched everyone around them eat with innocent glee, in the manner of children watching kittens lap at milk.

Dimity suggested to the vampires, in a mild tone, how nice it would be if they considered hosting some regular event or another for the neighborhood. Tea dueling, she had come to understand, was all the rage amongst young persons these days. Perhaps something along those lines? Or if that was too close to a village fete for comfort, simply opening up the house to regular visiting hours, so that the local gentry might pay calls upon them, should suffice.

Lord Kirby, of course, was against the idea instantly. For security reasons, if nothing else. But Dimity and Rosie, together, brought Lord Finbar round to the idea of perhaps a weekly artistic gathering or intellectual salon.

"You might give recitations?" suggested Dimity, with a tiny nod at Rosie, who instantly turned big pleading eyes on Lord Finbar. The girl was wasted on housework. Perhaps the War Office could use another agent?

Like the champ she was, Rosie picked up the gauntlet. "Oh dear me, yes, m'lord. You have a marvelous speaking voice. Do say you'll consider it?"

Lord Finbar said he would, indeed, consider it. And would Rosie like to hear some of his original poetry while she worked in the drawing room after tea?

Rosie said she very much would.

Dimity tried to give her a warning look.

But the bally girl only winked at Dimity and left, her tea half finished, duster spinning in a hypnotic manner. Lord Finbar followed her like an enthusiastic, if dour, basset hound.

Dimity distracted Lord Kirby from his open-mouthed shock at this exchange by relaying her concerns about the replacement window frame not exactly matching the rosettes of the old one and could he please lend his expert eye to such a serious matter?

He said he would be delighted and went with the carpenter to do so.

With tea completed and everyone mostly sorted, Dimity seized upon the opportunity to sneak down beneath the kitchen after Mr Theris and the missing milkmaid. Dimity wanted to see if she might pursue her actual primary objective of locating the missing hive queen.

Justice Wignall was a loon. Crispin could only stare in amazement. A very beautiful, very dramatic, but decidedly loony sort of loon. Cris felt a wave of affection wash over him. He was fond of loons. But this was taking things rather far, literally and figuratively.

The ethereal vampire ran the cold cobbles of downtown Nottingham so fast Cris was grateful for the general standards of his fitness regimen. Not fast by vampire standards, of course, more like a leisurely stroll for one of them, but fast for a human. Justice clearly wished to emphasize wafting over efficiency. The vampire was barefoot, the soft slap of his feet on the wet stone echoing through the streets. Nottingham was a lace-making city, and lace required good lighting, so the place was – by industry and nature – mostly composed of daylight folk. Nights were relatively quiet for a large urban town, especially to a man like Cris, who'd always made his home in London amongst the Progressive Set. So while there were a few people about and evening enterprises and tradesmen working away, it was nowhere like the hustle and bustle of old London Town.

If Justice was aware of Sir Crispin shadowing him, he didn't show it. Honestly, how could he not be aware? Crispin's boots positively *clopped*. He might be fit, but he was no expert on running long distances in inappropriate garb. What worried Cris was the distance. Generally speaking, hive-bound vampires, especially young ones like Justice, had to remain within a few blocks of their queen at all times. As they got older they could go farther away, and the queen's praetoriani, by necessity, had a large range of motion. The fact that Justice could even leave city limits was worrisome. The queen's hold to his tether was clearly weakening. And a vampire's tether only stretched so far until it snapped.

They eventually reached some kind of unkempt park, and within that, some species of coppice or diminutive wooded area.

No doubt this was the objective, for Justice slowed and began a dramatic stumbling run, arms flailing gracefully – artlessly lost and forlorn in the vast forest (of two dozen or so trees, mind you). The stolen white nightgown trailed behind the vampire, pulling along loose leaves and branches. The hem dampened. A sleeve caught and tore.

Cris worried about Dimity's reaction.

Finally Justice cast himself dramatically down

upon the roots of a massive oak tree. He arranged himself to look like some painting out of the Pre-Raphaelite Brotherhood. Sir Crispin felt that Justice might be going for an interpretation of Tennyson's appalling poem, *Lady of Shalott.*

Cris hid behind a scruffy shrub and waited to see what might happen next. Above him, through the branches and occasional cloud, the night sky twinkled. Cris took a brief moment to appreciate seeing the stars once more. It had been so long.

A gentleman came riding through the coppice and dismounted with the ease of one truly comfortable in the saddle. He was dressed for the hunt – red jacket, tight cream-colored jodhpurs, a high top hat, and a crop in his hand.

He clearly was not hunting foxes, however.

The man was on the stout side, of the kind that would go comfortably to chubby in his twilight years. His face was wide and ruddy, with a pronounced divot in the chin and an impressive set of whiskers.

"Justice, my own, my love... How beautiful and tragic you look."

Justice leaned up on one arm and beckoned him over. "Oh Gantry, my dearest treasure, I am overwrought."

This, then, must be the lover, Gantry Ogdon-Loppes. For surely Nottingham boasted only one *Gantry.*

The Gantry in question stumbled over a root, and eased himself down to one knee – no doubt a challenge in such tight trousers – to bend over the prostrate vampire.

"Come into my strong arms that I may cherish you."
He caught the vampire up and clasped him to his chest.

Justice flopped about in what was no doubt *meant*
to be a faint of overwhelming emotion, but which
looked remarkably dead-fish-like.

The moon cast a thin, reedy light through a break
in the clouds above. This made Justice glow pale as
the underbelly of said fish.

"I say, you are quite the finest of fillies!" Gantry
was no doubt going off script with that statement, but
his admiration sounded genuine.

Really, it was quite the performance. Cris wondered
if they were taking advantage of his presence, or if they
always acted this way with one another. In which
case... measures would need to be taken.

Justice turned about and clutched Gantry's ruddy
checks in perfect lily-white hands. "Oh, but I have
missed you so. The day spent sleeping alone seemed
an eternity."

"Then let me come to you! Beg your queen."

Queen? That was interesting. It meant Justice was
out to Gantry as a vampire.

"We never see her anymore, she has rejected the
world. I am unmoored. I have only you, my darling,
while we await her return," Justice intoned.

Gantry pressed, "Then you must take me into your
hive so that I may hold you and we may weather this
storm together. I will be your succor."

"But your parents!"

"Hang my parents! They'll come around. If I could
but tell them of your unnatural state. Become your
drone and love in truth."

"But my queen! She sees no one, ever. She has locked herself away from the world. How can I ask? She will not allow me into her presence."

"How could anyone possibly deny you? My own, my dearest! Who would not want to gaze upon your beauty? You will make her see reason. We are meant to be together. I am meant to be beside you, always and forever, day or night."

"Oh Gantry, you are too good for me. So handsome, so delicious." Justice's fangs gleamed.

Crispin honestly couldn't take any more of it. He'd learned all he needed. Gantry was willing to turn drone. His parents had made some objection to the match, but they did not know drone was on offer. Justice was feeding on a willing lover. This was enough information to be going on with – he needn't torture his ears any further.

He'd tell all to Dimity, for she would no doubt know the way to go about setting this to rights. And she ought to know what crimes of sentimentality had been committed while wearing her night-rail.

Dimity explored the kitchen, finding nothing of any import and no apparent exit. Where had Mr Theris gone to fetch the milkmaid?

She was near to giving up when she found what could only be a trap door in the middle of the scullery floor. One no doubt originally intended to lead into a root cellar.

Cook gave her an expressive look but was clearly

one to mind her own business, which currently involved putting away the remnants of tea.

Dimity opened the door. Instead of a ladder, the door opened onto a set of narrow stairs cut into the limestone, which extended down so far into the darkness, it was impossible to see where they ended.

Dimity climbed down with alacrity, holding her skirts high, and feeling very daring. The stairs led to a perfectly respectable tunnel (once her eyes adjusted to the gloom). It was the kind used by breweries to store beer barrels, except longer. At the far end of it was a door. As she approached, making no noise with her soft slippers and trained to be silent, she heard arguing coming from behind it.

A strong, cultured female voice was saying, "After what was done to me, how can I show my face again?"

Mr Theris's voice came then, tone soothing, murmuring calm words and platitudes.

"Never!" was the reply. "Now you must leave me, Cinjin. For everyone does, in the end."

The door creaked open. Dimity caught a glimpse of a rail-thin woman with red hair and a black brocade tea gown before Mr Theris and the milkmaid, now pale and punctured, came through.

Dimity leaned against the cold limestone wall, feeling a little faint. The punctures appeared deeper and more bloody than last time. She pressed her clammy forehead to the stone, closed her eyes, and took a few deep breaths.

Mr Theris shut the door loudly behind him. Dimity opened her eyes. The actor was glaring at her.

"What are you doing down here, Mrs Carefull?"

"You mean this isn't where the extra embroidery samples are kept? I felt sure you must have more, and I thought a display in the study..."

Mr Theris shook his head at her, exasperated. "You're almost entirely composed of belters, aren't you, Mrs Carefull? If that's even your name. You may be as good an actor as I, but I know your kind. Now go on back. You know I can't leave you down here without permission or supervision." His eyes were cold. She was once more imposing on his domain.

"But if I could only ask the hive queen..."

"No, Mrs Carefull, upstairs with you. Haven't you done enough damage already?" He turned and locked the door behind him with a large key. Certainly even a door as thickly bolted as that one could not confine a vampire queen, so the locking was for Dimity's benefit. It was designed to keep others out, not trap the baroness. Dimity thought the lock looked very hard and solid and difficult to pick, but she might be able to steal that key.

She sighed and turned to lead the way back though the limestone tunnel and up the stone steps. She helped the milkmaid into the scullery and they both brushed off their skirts.

Mr Theris closed the trap door with a decided snap, and then retrieved a steak and kidney pie from the scullery, ignoring Cook's glare. He had a decorated lace Valentine's card in his free hand. He ushered the milkmaid before him to the entranceway, where he thanked her with the silver coin payment, the pie, and the card.

Once the milkmaid was away, Dimity turned back

to Mr Theris, who was looking around at the now clean entranceway, bare of pictures, furniture, and rugs. Two spry young men were re-papering it in a delightful royal blue pattern depicting peacocks and silver eggs, which Dimity thought would set off the mahogany railing quite nicely.

Dimity sidled up to Mr Theris, eyes big as she could make them. Time to try a different tactic.

He looked skeptical and then leering, clearly ready to play her game. "Mrs Carefull, be cautious now. I'm easily susceptible to the fairer sex."

"Are you, indeed, Mr Theris?" Dimity doubted her skills when up against this angry rake, but she also wanted answers.

"Cinjin, please." He puffed out his chest and took a fencer's stance.

"Cinjin." She trailed a finger up his sleeve. "Not too susceptible? She upset you?"

"She refused my counsel. She always refuses. She thinks I'm a child who could not possibly understand her."

"When clearly you are a man with only her best interests at heart. Why is she so reluctant to take solace in her hive? What was done to her?"

Mr Theris shook his head, covering her hand with his and making a good examination of the neckline of her dress. It was too high to see down, although she made a note to activate her décolletage should she need to distract this man in future.

Then he reached forward and began to twiddle with the top button of her bodice.

Right there in the hallway.

Really, it was too much. She was actually rather shocked.

Dimity tittered at him and turned away. "Really, Mr Theris, there are people about."

"Then let us go upstairs." His eyes narrowed. He was pushing her to see how far she would take things.

"But the queen – I'm dying to know. What was done to her?"

Mr Theris tried to turn her back to face him again. "Something fashion-related, I understand. Kirby knows." He reached up to toy with her top button again and then ran two fingers down from one button to the next, bump bump bump, over her chest towards her belt.

"Why, Mr Theris, how rude you are. Stop that this minute!"

The hand continued.

Dimity considered her options. This was not a subtle man, which meant, unfortunately, that violence was likely best. With a small sigh, she extracted the muff pistol that always lived in the depths of her right skirt seam, in a hidden pocket there.

He didn't notice. He was watching his own hand sweep down her front.

Dimity raised her gun, pointing it up his not insubstantial nose. "Look here, Mr Theris. I don't want to shoot you, but I will if I must. You see, if I shoot you, there will be blood. It's terribly embarrassing, but when I see blood, I have a propensity to faint. And you wouldn't notice because you would be dead, but I would be most awfully inconvenienced. Not to mention this lovely new wallpaper would be spattered. So if you would kindly keep your hands to yourself... there's a good chap."

"Why, Mrs Carefull, you have a gun. Are lady painters supposed to carry guns?"

"Around you, Mr Theris, apparently all ladies should carry guns."

"Did I misread you, Mrs Carefull?"

"I love my husband, Mr Theris."

"What does that have to do with anything?"

The front door opened then, without a knock, and Sir Crispin came in, bringing with him the sounds and scents of heavy rain. It must have started while they were in the limestone caves. "Really, I begin to think Nottingham is one big puddle." He paused in the act of removing his greatcoat, noting the tête-à-tête before him with a raised eyebrow. "What's all this, then?"

Mr Theris backed away from Dimity. She found it aggravating that he was more afraid of Sir Crispin than of her pistol. Dimity stashed the gun back in its secret pocket, while the drone was otherwise occupied in looking at her enraged husband.

Sir Crispin did look angry. In that quiet fierce way that meant *real* anger, not the simulated kind.

Oh dear.

"Were you *touching* my wife, sir?"

CHAPTER SIX

Dangerous Buttons

Cris noted everything all at once. The bally actor's hands all over his Sparkles. Her face – whiter than usual. The tiny gun in her hand – steady.

If she hadn't had the gun out, he would still have been angry, but he would have assumed she was working to extract something from Mr Bloody Theris. Cris would have played it off with bluster and confusion, the bumbling husband with delusions of fidelity.

But she looked genuinely frightened and he'd been concerned about the drone from the get-go. Theris was the kind of man who took any offer of friendship as encouragement, for whom all flirtation was encoded seduction. A man who had to prove himself as male through the domination of others, whatever form that took. Dimity might be the intelligencer, but Crispin knew all too well the depths of male depravity. His own father was an ideal model of the species. Mr Theris was a spoiled child to whom no one had ever said no, and those kinds of boys became immeasurably dangerous men. And now, there stood Sparkles with her pistol pointed.

Or not. The pistol had vanished.

Dimity swept towards him. "Now, now, husband, darling, never you worry. Mr Theris and I were just coming to an understanding."

"Were you indeed?" He made his arms go languid, cat-like, and pulled his frame up from the middle of the back at the same time, so those few inches he had on the actor were that much more evident.

Dimity made a shooing motion at Mr Theris. The drone took that as a courtesy and left with alacrity.

"Let him go," Dimity murmured. "I want him scared and confused. He'll make mistakes."

"Have you figured his game yet?"

"Dependency. He wants to be the only one they lean on. He orchestrated the removal of servants and fellow drones, I'm certain of it. Already he is nervous since I've brought back staff. Also, he sees us as possible new drones, as threats. Soon, I think, he will show his hand."

"Will he take drastic or violent measures?"

"I don't think so. He didn't kill the others. Just got them sent away. He wants all the attention. Actor, you see? But I'm pushing him to his limit. I've discovered that he keeps the key to the queen's cave on him." She looked around furtively. The front entrance was, for the moment, empty but for them. Deftly, she showed him something in her hand – a large, old-fashioned key. "Or he did."

Unwilling to discuss it openly, he only nodded and finished sliding out of his greatcoat to hang it in the coat room.

Dimity squeaked. "You're still in a bathing costume!"

He glowered at her. "It's pouring out there. Seemed appropriate."

"Where did your expedition take you?"

"Let's go upstairs. I like the new wallpaper, by the way."

"Thank you." She led the way up to their room.

Once she strummed up the harmonic auditory resonance disruptor, he felt more comfortable talking openly.

Cris took a deep breath and tilted his head back, rolling the sudden kinks from his neck, and asked a question that really worried him. "You planning on using that key right away?"

Dimity shook her head. "No indeed, I've more groundwork to lay before I approach the queen. I want this house spruced up in the extreme, immeasurably alluring. No, I think you should go out and get a copy made, please. Tonight, if possible. Then I'll toss it into in his room, as if it fell out of his pocket. Best he not know we have access to the baroness."

"Crafty Sparkles." Crispin didn't say how uncomfortable he found the idea of her having direct access to a possibly insane vampire queen, because she'd likely take that as criticism or doubt in her capabilities. Really, it was simply that he worried about her.

"You sure you're well, Sparkles? He didn't hurt you? Anything inappropriate?"

"The man is fascinated with my buttons." She gestured casually to the ones that trailed down the front of her formidable figure.

"Oh, I say!" Cris was suddenly intent on finding

Mr Theris and doing something unpleasantly manipulative to his limbs. "Buttons, is it? I'll teach him about bally buttons."

"Yes dear, yes, of course you *could*. But we might use it to our advantage. Not right now. Please stop fussing."

That bit of fear he'd seen in her eyes, if indeed it was honest, was long gone. Now he was beginning to second-guess what he thought he'd seen, which was one of her tricks, of course – playing with his mind as well as everyone else's. "I don't like that you felt it necessary to pull out your pistol. How many times have I been your safety over the years? You've never used a gun before."

"Never needed to. Not my preferred weapon – so loud and messy. Does it expose us too much, do you think, my brandishing it at that horrible man?" Dimity checked that the door was tightly closed, then wedged one of the chairs against it.

"You explained how you came to have one?"

"After a fashion."

Cris shrugged. He was far more concerned that she had felt desperate enough to brandish it. "I suspect the hive no longer thinks of us as *simple* artists. You, at least, have a talent for household management and the arrangement of furnishings."

"The three vampires seem remarkably undeterred by my highhandedness."

"Vampires are probably accustomed to being managed by drones and staff. Like most aristocrats, vampires rarely concern themselves with earthly matters. Only Theris seems to be noticing and minding all the activity."

"I will manage him too, I promise. Do stop fretting."

"I'm not!"

"You're pacing. And not your normal thoughtful kind of pacing. This is your anger-stride pacing. The room is hardly big enough."

He was. While she was perched calmly on the edge of the bed, watching him.

"He frightened you."

"A little, or I wouldn't have resorted to the gun. But I suspect he is of the type that would not take any other threat from a woman to heart. I mean, I could have used a knee, or a small knife. A gun is awfully crude. But then, so is Mr Theris."

"That man!" Cris tensed and forced himself to stop striding about.

"He is accustomed to being irresistible. So am I. It was never going to be a good combination, unless I actually let him seduce me." She gave a delicate shudder. "No, thank you."

"But did you *get* anything?"

"Aside from the key? Actually, yes. The queen's distress and resulting withdrawal appears to be fashion based and apparently Lord Kirby knows the particulars."

Cris was impressed enough to stop pacing and stare at her.

She folded her hands in her lap demurely. "And I know exactly where the baroness has been hiding and how to get at her. *And* I'm considering an extraction plan once Theris is out of the way."

"Bloody hell."

"Exactly."

"You're brilliant, aren't you?" He couldn't help it, drawn to her coy pride. He bent and curved one hand about her soft cheek.

She grinned into the caress. "I have my moments. And what about you? I can't imagine you went voluntarily into the streets of Nottingham dressed like a beachcomber, greatcoat or no greatcoat. You were following Justice?"

"I was." He lowered his hand and sat next to her – not too close, he didn't want to crowd, the memory of Theris's disgusting behaviour still fresh in his mind. But she wouldn't let him be far away. She pressed against him, copious skirts spilling over his leg.

"And?" She bumped his shoulder with hers.

Cris described what he'd seen and heard, ending on Gantry's apparent willingness to turn drone. "Although his parents seem to object to the match. I can't imagine they would if they knew Justice is a vampire. Not if they're progressives. Gantry is a younger son and clearly bent enough not to get a continuation of the family line out of his loins. Drone is an ideal result. The parents should be approached with a blood-dowry, unless they have a reputation for anti-integration."

Dimity shook her head. "Not just yet. Even I'm not that highhanded. We haven't that kind of authority – that's beyond housekeeping or estate management. The queen has to approve a hive reveal, let alone a new drone contract. We aren't there yet." She gestured with the key she still held.

Cris nodded. She was right, of course. He was getting ahead of himself and he had such faith in her abilities. Indeed, it seemed, given the rapidly reviving state of Budgy Hall, that his Sparkles could do anything.

Dimity pursed her lips. "It's possible this Gantry fellow is smarter than you think and knows Justice well enough to have invented a parental impediment specifically in order to cultivate the vampire's interest. Added dramatic effect, if you will?"

"Crickets! You see, Sparkles, this is why you're the intelligencer and I'm the safety. How are the rest of the hive coming along?"

"Vampires are tricky, but I think I need to give them purpose, an event of some kind, show off the hive house. An excuse to throw a gathering, invite the local gentry, including the Ogdon-Loppeses. The kind of high-society event that no one who is anyone wants to miss. Least of all the baroness. And I need to take Justice shopping. Can't have a vampire stealing my nightgown every time he wants to go trysting in a forest. I only brought the one."

She looked at Cris, suddenly serious. "It's interesting that you're so comfortable with him. In my experience, men of your type are not comfortable around men of his."

"Justice?" He wondered what she meant by *his type,* but he could guess what she meant by Justice's.

"Yes." She was looking at the key in her hands, fiddling with it.

"Reminds me of my brother." He stopped her fingers around the metal, squeezed gently. He was usually the twitchy one. Somehow, though, this made him feel calm, her being nervous about his reactions – he didn't mind telling her of his past. She'd never judge. She wasn't remotely like that. She'd judge a man's throw pillows, but not his family.

"You have a brother? That's not in your records. Sisters, yes, but no brother." Her eyes were earnest.

"You've read my records. Of course you have." Cris felt that funny lump at the base of his throat that always materialized when he thought of Tristan. "He died."

"Oh, how sad. I am sorry. Was it an accident?"

It was not a comfortable matter for him to explain. But suddenly it seemed important that she know. Because it was part of what made him a safety, part of what made him so comfortable around Bertie and Mrs Bagley and their eccentric relationships, even vampires. Part of what made him... him.

"Not precisely. I adored him, actually. The world was not so kind. Our father was a brute to the poor kid." Cris had tried to protect Tristan. Tried so hard. But he was only a kid himself, Tristan's elder by only a year and a half, and his father had been so big and so angry all the time.

"Oh! Oh. He was *exactly* like Justice then? Women's clothes and everything?"

Cris nodded. "And terribly fragile." He felt his lips twisting, so he pressed them together as hard as he could, trying to battle the lump in his throat into submission. "He did love it so. All the frills and lace. He was so happy to have sisters. He's the youngest, you see, after me. Or he was. They used to dress him up like a doll. Before we were told off for it." He let himself feel the fondness. The love that was the foundation of the lump. Tristan had been the sweetest child in the world. Always helping the maids, or the cooks, always willing to fuss with a sister's hair. He loved to be given household tasks, arranging the flowers or setting the table. Used to follow Cris around like a little puppy when Cris was home from Eton, sit next to him, rest his head on Crispin's shoulder.

Dimity moved even closer to him, placed a tentative hand on his thigh, pushed warm satin and lemon scent against his discomfort. He let himself hope that, if she knew how much he wanted it, she'd climb right into his lap. It made the lump hurt more that she understood his need for touch right now.

"Now the sisters are always trying to marry me off. I think they're afraid I might turn out like him." He leaned into her strength.

"Oh, but you're, you know..." She gestured with her chin, up and down, still close. "You. Not at all, uh... frail?"

He felt himself give a shaky smile. "Not like that. Not worried that I'm after their stockings and fans either. He hanged himself, you see."

Dimity shuddered against him. Gave a sad little whimper. "Oh, I'm so sorry, how awful."

"It was a long time ago now."

She looked up at him, close and fierce. "It never stops hurting, though, does it? They say it will, but it's always there. You don't stop missing the people you loved. Maybe you can heal from losing *things,* but not *people*. They take a bit of your soul with them and that's not a wound that ever mends completely. It's not a ghost, but the absence of one."

She wrested one little hand free of his grip. He hadn't even realized he'd done that – taken both her hands and the key into his.

She touched his cheek, soft and sure. Her mouth firmed. "I won't let anything bad happen to Justice, I promise. I mean, he's immortal, so that's not so much of a concern. But I'll get him settled and happy. I'll get them all that way. You see if I don't. Despite themselves." She paused then. "Except Mr Theris. He's on his own. My teacher used to say there are some people who simply can't be taught. I think he's one of them. But he *can* be relocated." Her eyes gleamed.

Strangely, this did reassure Crispin. Helped a bit. Reminded him there was work to do and that they were in this together.

"And here I was meant to be consoling you."

Dimity sniffed and stuck her pert little nose in the air. "Not the first time a man has been tempted by my buttons. Certainly won't be the last, I'll warrant."

That reminded him he was annoyed at Mr Theris, which was so much easier than being sad, so he grabbed on to it. "I wish it were the last."

"Do you? What a nice thing to say. I suspect I'd have to give up Honey Beeing for that to be the case." She rested her head on his upper arm.

"Have you considered it? Not that I don't think you're a wonderful intelligencer." He wanted to hope, but hardly dared.

"I know I'm good, but do I even like it anymore?" Her thumb caressed the seam of his stupid striped exercise suit. They were angled towards each other now where they sat on the bed.

"Do you?" He focused on the wistfulness in her eyes. Did she want more excitement, or less? Did she want something entirely different?

"Not really. I like the bit where I get to pick out wallpaper and order people to make things beautiful. I like the bit where I can tidy up messy lives and enforce contentment."

"You could be a *grande dame* of high society and still do all of that." He felt a kind of roar in his ears, blood rushing – hope.

"Yes, I could, couldn't I? I considered it. Arranging a wealthy, highly situated husband for myself. Maybe even a kind and decent one, who'd actually love me. Does that seem trite?" She looked away as if she were ashamed of having small dreams. But her one hand, holding the key, remained clasped in his. "This wasn't what I wanted originally, did you know? Espionage. It was simply that my parents insisted and now all my dearest friends do it and they love it so. I thought I could help and serve my country and be useful. I have the training. I'm pretty good at certain missions. So why not? And now I'm rather stuck."

"So busy fixing others' lives, you forgot about your own?" He wasn't wealthy or highly situated but he thought he'd be very good at loving her, if he were given a chance.

She sniffed. "Well, possibly. And what about you? Are you happy being safety to silly girls, with no silly girl of your own? What's your excuse?"

"Tristan, I suppose. Trying to improve matters. And my father – stopping men like him. Over and over, simply *stopping* them. I think, both you and I, we want to make the world better for others. You want them happy. I want them safe."

"We both ended up a little lonely, though, as a result. I think I did, anyway." She sounded so sad and she was still so close. But with the memory of horrible Mr Theris still fresh in Crispin's mind, he didn't, wouldn't, do anything to break the surety she found in his presence.

It seemed she was not so reluctant. "I feel safe with you, have I ever said as much? Does that help? I mean to say, I know you grump at me and you think me frivolous."

"I think you're wonderful."

But she was getting started on one of her chatterings. "I am, of course. Frivolous, I mean. Because I really do think the right pair of gloves could save the world, if applied properly. But I'm also well aware gloves don't solve everything, not even the *right* pair. So it might not be such a reassuring thing, coming from me. But I'm not playing with you, I'm really not. I haven't batted my lashes in your direction even once. Not intentionally. Because you *are* kind, and I think you might be good and decent too. So I wouldn't do that to you. You know that, right? I don't want you to be one of the men manipulated by the Honey Bee. Do you see?"

"Yes, Sparkles, I see." And the rushing hope in his ears crashed over him, and he went from yearning for something he thought he'd never have, to wanting what was right there, sitting next to him.

"Oh well, good. Uh, quite." She paused. "Would you kiss me then, sometime? If you liked? Or I could kiss you. So long as you didn't think it was me being too much Honey Bee? Only I've rarely got that far and I don't think I'm very good at it, so I'd prefer it if you started."

Cris understood, then, what her fear was. What kept her dancing about him, unsure. She had no idea how to cope with inadequacy. He, on the other hand, felt that way most of the time around her. But in this matter, at least, he had the upper hand. He left her holding the key and cupped her face with both hands, stilling her mouth with his – soft and brief and sweet, like sipping nectar.

"You're you and you're also the Honey Bee, and I like them both."

"Oh really? That's good, that's very good, isn't it? Kiss me again?"

So he did.

Dimity had been kissed properly at last. He was good at it too, and she was pleased to have found herself an expert on the matter. She wasn't one to begrudge his experience, especially when she was the one to benefit from it. They'd done nothing more than kiss, sweet but sure, because Cris needed to change and go find a locksmith, and she needed to supervise tradesfolk, flatter vampires, and pretend to paint more frolicking cows.

Just before sunrise, when they eventually sought their bed, Sir Crispin touched her at last. More than simply a kiss, this time.

Dimity was delighted that he took the chance, finally. As if she hadn't been trying to get him to do something similar since the very first night, silly man. His wide hands were gentle, and more reassuring than anything, simply tucking her close to him. He did nothing more than smooth down her back, stroking over the chemisette and petticoat that she had to wear – because Justice hadn't returned her peignoir.

"Honestly, it's one thing to borrow a lady's nightgown to enact a theatrical woodland love story. I mean, what lady of sentiment wouldn't loan out her night-rail for such use? But it's quite another not to return it afterwards." She said this in mock affront, feeling the tingle that his stroking hands left behind and trying to work up the courage to do some exploring of her own.

"I'm afraid it got rather torn and muddy, returned or not." He turned his head into her hair. He was always touching it, eager to brush it for her, eager to inhale the scent. She was flattered. She'd always been rather proud of her hair, having grown it herself, as it were.

"Well, I hope it gets a good cleaning, then." She finally marshalled enough courage to run her hand over his chest, the thin fabric of his shirt doing little to hide the texture of the chest hair underneath, the warmth, the firm bumps of ribs and swells of muscle.

"What you have on now is lovely, with less material." Crispin's voice was a rumble of appreciation as his hand curved around her waist, pressing the loose material of the chemisette against her. An odd sensation – no one had ever really touched her there before. Her skin tingled slightly, pinpricked by pleasure.

"Is that good?" She let her hand trail down to his stomach, which clenched under it.

"Possibly too good, Sparkles. I'm a gentleman." He put his hand atop hers to stop its wandering any farther down. While she really wanted to explore farther, she was also a little relieved he'd stopped her.

"Yes, but could we kiss more?" That was something she already knew she loved.

"Lying down in bed together? That would test my control something fierce. Just stay here against me."

"But more would be nice." She could still tease, couldn't she? He had said he liked both Dimity and the Honey Bee.

"Hum." He rumbled in amusement under her cheek. "Yes, it would. But perhaps when we aren't on a mission, infiltrating a vampire hive?"

"You're sure?" That was a week and a half away! An awfully long time to wait. Especially as she was feeling flushed and aching in a way that she was certain he could fix.

"Not at all. I would love to ravish you."

"You would? How delightful." That was very good information to have. "I've waited a long time to be ravished by a tuppenny knight."

"A what?" he rumbled, half in amusement, half in offence.

Dimity giggled. "I once told my true friends –

you'll meet them some day, I promise – I once told them, even though we were training to kill things at the time, that all I really wanted was marriage and maybe children with some tuppenny knight. You know, a gentleman of only modest means and minimal importance. Like you."

"I thought you wanted wealth and social standing?"

"Oh no, I said I thought I *could* be a society dragon, if I wanted it. But honestly? Simply a tuppenny knight. Perhaps one inclined towards politics. Then I could throw political soirees." These were half-formed dreams, inconsequential. But he would be good at politics and it was another way to help people, another way to keep them safe.

He did not stop stroking her, which seemed a good sign. "Tuppenny knight, hm? I don't know exactly how I feel about that. Somehow I feel I've just been both insulted and complimented."

"It's decidedly a compliment. Gentlemen of gross means and maximum importance are utterly intolerable."

"So I, then, I'm that knight – that wish you told your true friends?"

Dimity breathed into courage. "Yes," she whispered.

"Is that a proposal, Sparkles?"

Dimity's breath caught. Was it? Did she really want that small, slight future – with him? Oh, yes. She really, really did. But was she allowed such a gift? Did she get to have her childhood dream, those funny flippant hopes of youth? Had she earned the right to leave intelligence behind? Could she be that lucky? Could anyone?

It was dangerous to hope for such a thing, but Dimity knew danger. "Would you be interested, if it were?"

He kissed the top of her head. She wished it were lower down, but she wasn't going to press. Not when they'd already had one epiphany tonight. At least he didn't seem repulsed by the banality of her imagined future.

"It sounds absolutely lovely." He brushed his chin through her hair. His face had been made rough by the passing of hours and it caught on the fine strands.

"Excellent," said Dimity, flushed with heat and victory. "But fix the hive first?"

"Yes, Sparkles, hive first." He settled then, relaxed and still against her. Still as he so rarely was, even in sleep – warm and reassuring.

Dimity dozed off, thinking about the fact that he'd been calling her Sparkles for years. She'd thought it was a criticism – of the way she chattered and her propensity for bright colors and shiny jewelry. But now she suspected that it had been an endearment all along.

The next evening, just prior to sunset, Dimity awoke refreshed and ready to make the most of a new night. She was dressed and out of bed before Crispin, but not out of any sense of discomfort or awkwardness. In fact, she felt a new sensation of proprietary closeness towards the man.

Her knight. Hers.

She watched him with open and obvious interest
when he got out of bed and stretched in his nightshirt,
lean muscles and legs on display. He gave her a
cheeky grin as he walked into the dressing room to
conduct his ablutions, and she turned to blatantly
admire his calves.

She'd decided, at some point while they slept, that
she would touch him if she liked. He seemed reluctant
to take the initial approach, but eager enough once he
was certain of her positive reception. Something held
him back. Too much a gentleman, or too afraid of
giving offence. So, she would touch him first and
often. He seemed delighted to let this happen.

She asked, of course, when he returned to the
bedroom, pulling on his waistcoat. Asked if it might
be all right, since they weren't going to do anything
more than kiss, not yet anyway, if she could maybe
pet him a bit?

He replied, with a grave face, trying to hide a
smile, that he thought he was man enough to
withstand it.

She said this was excellent and that he should do
the same. At which his face fell and he muttered
something about buttons and Mr Theris, and his father
(who apparently was quite the rake and took
advantage of very young ladies). Dimity impressed
upon him that this was an entirely different matter.
And that Cris was no rake and could fiddle with her
buttons anytime they were alone, as much as he liked.

He said he wasn't that kind of chap.

She said she certainly hoped he was!

Then he said, yes, he *was* the kind of chap who wanted to see beyond the buttons, so to speak, but only if she really wanted that.

She stood up from the vanity, her hair done, and offered to undo the buttons herself, right then and there, to prove her point. She was wearing a golden brown dress with a great deal of cream fringe this evening, and a suite of gold and pearl jewelry, which boasted metallic fringe on the brooch, earrings, and hair comb. The dress had tiny buttons all down the front, and she meant what she'd said about them, too.

He took one big step towards her and lifted her up, and cuddled her close, and kissed all over her face with little soft pecks. She giggled like a mad thing.

After that they were both breathing hard, and she could feel all of him against her in ways she'd heard of, and read of, but never really experienced. She wiggled a bit, experimentally. And he groaned into her neck.

"Good," she said, pleased with herself and her newfound knowledge, and the certain power this gave her over him. Pleased in a way that was probably a little bit too much Honey Bee. But honestly, a lady liked to know she could interest the gentleman of her affections in all ways – upstairs and downstairs, so to speak.

At least Dimity liked to. Because she was that kind of lady. She wanted carnal relations to be good and work well between them. Her true friend Sophronia had told her of such things and what to expect and why it was important. And Sophronia should know, since she'd been sinfully enamoured of, and sharing a bed with, an entirely inappropriate and perfectly wonderful man for many years.

Cris put her down.

"You have excellent control," said Dimity, looking him over – all over, feeling hungry for something not sustenance.

"Not so excellent that I can withstand your looking at me like that."

"I'm going to test it," she vowed. Feeling very brave and having been given permission, she reached for his gentleman's parts, and cupped him there, softly and carefully.

"Oh, crickets," said Sir Crispin. His big body shuddered and he twitched in her hand.

Dimity felt hot and powerful, only slightly terrified, and very eager. "Oh my," she said, having lost her chatter in surprise at the warmth and hardness and how much it made her want more. "I have to, uh, go, I think, now, before I can't."

With which she waltzed out, because there were things the Honey Bee needed to accomplish, and Dimity's desires would have to wait a bit longer. Then she waltzed back in, in time to catch Sir Crispin adjusting himself and looking uncomfortable. Which was delightful.

"Oh, and Cris, dear?"

"Yes, Sparkles?" he said on a long sigh, voice sandy.

"I've a shopping list for you. Be a love and go into town for me first thing?"

"Of course, dear."

She blew him a kiss.

"You're going to be a terror, aren't you?"

She waggled her eyebrows at him, feeling tremendously pleased with herself. "If you're very, very lucky."

He groaned happily, and she trotted back out, about her plans and schemes.

Dimity's list was extensive and it kept Crispin dashing about collecting packages, and ordering more stuff, and posting letters, and such like for positively *hours*. There was a list of very specific items that a town like Nottingham could provide, but only after much effort and expense.

She had these noted in a neat hand:

Absolutely Vital:

1. Trouve automated rotating chamois.

2. Any leather-bound volume by Ralph Waldo Emerson, poetry preferred, similar forward-thinking American authors also acceptable.

3. A London playbill, something bold, successful, and recent, e.g. The Phantom of Bedlam's Bottom.

4. Parisian fashion plates, Spring 1869 only.

5. Something frilly, pretty, and colorful – shawl perhaps? Use best judgement.

6. Additional gentlemen's ballet attire, perhaps not striped, but still tight, for you, of course – remember your adoring public.

Cris did his best, but it took longer than he expected. He also retrieved the newly pressed key, not liking the danger it represented but knowing she was, in fact, good at her job.

He returned in time for midnight tea, which had apparently become a tradition. Dimity had gathered everyone, from hive to new staff to visiting tradesfolk, in the dining room. There the humans were eating and the three vampires were holding court.

Lord Finbar was bending the ear of Rosie, one of the new parlormaids. Or Cris thought that was her name. He was waxing poetical about something and she was looking up at him raptly, showing off the long slim column of her neck. Lord Finbar was still tortured by the woes of the world, but he was also clearly enjoying telling her all about his torment. In great detail.

Lord Kirby was in animated discussion with a carpenter and an upholsterer about the interrelationship of wood and fabric. His silver hair was pulled back in a loose knot and his medieval robes appeared to be dark blue tonight rather than black, both an improvement on his original appearance. Unfortunately, the robe was still velvet. But as Dimity would say, these things took time.

Justice was there too, sitting next to Dimity and engaging in what appeared to be a long argument on the nature of color choices, contrast versus complementary, and what they said about a person's vital humors.

Cris walked in, acquired a cup of tea, and sat down nearby in time to hear Dimity say, "I find whites very challenging, don't you, Justice darling? They attract bits of dust and stray smudges so easily. I should so love to see you in color. White does so – for lack of a better term – *whitewash* you out." She turned to the plasterer. "No offense, Mr Headicar. Honestly, Justice sweetie, your complexion is so wonderfully pale already. Don't you think blue would set it off beautifully?"

Justice looked intrigued. "Blue is Gantry's favorite color."

"There, you see, I knew blue would suit. Shall we go shopping together? Tomorrow night perhaps? My husband is so busy about his dance practice and his errands, I should love to have you as an escort. We could look at night attire as well, find something frilly."

Justice hung his head only a little at the gentle dig. "Yes, I believe I owe you a new night-rail."

Dimity was clearly embarrassed to have such an intimate item mentioned at tea, but no one except Cris was listening to their conversation. "Yes, my dear, you might." She lowered her voice conspiratorially and nodded towards Cris. "I believe my husband has expressed an interest in something comprising *less* material."

Justice looked with wide delighted eyes between them. "Then may I...?"

Dimity nodded. "You may keep that one. But shopping is still in our future." She evaluated Justice's piratical white floppy shirt. "Perhaps something a bit more fitted?"

Justice looked down at himself. "But I'm so thin."

"You're svelte, darling!" Dimity protested. "You simply need the right cut and we shall see you for the perfect petite flower that you are. Gantry will adore it, I promise."

Justice nodded, still wide-eyed. "Blue... You're certain?"

"Without question," Dimity sipped her tea gravely and nodded, then turned sparkling eyes on Sir Crispin. "Now, husband, have you brought me everything I asked for?"

Cris knew a cue when he heard one. He finished his own tea, stood and came about to peck her on the cheek. "Of course, dear heart. I think I might practice next tonight, if there's space for me? I left your packages in the hall." He slipped her the old key and the copy, an easy exchange in her lap beneath the tablecloth.

She grasped easily onto their artist personas. "Yes, you should, and I will play for you again. Did you find something less striped?"

"Yes, I believe it should suffice. There's very little ready-made sportswear hereabouts."

"Lace abounds, but not much else, I'm afraid."

Justice agreed, grave. "Nottingham is, fashionably speaking, sadly behind the times."

Dimity shrugged. "If we must send to London, we must, but I think we can make do. The sitting room should suffice for your use this evening, my dear. Would you bring me the automated chamois you acquired, please, before you change?"

Cris left to do as requested, returning with a fancy box labeled *Trouve* in big swirling letters.

Dimity took it from him with a grin, then passed it over to Lord Kirby. "Lord Kirby, this is for you."

The vampire looked truly surprised, as though no one had ever given him a gift before. It was possible it had been a long while – as patrons, vampires often gave gifts, but rarely received them. He opened it as if the box itself were something quite precious and extracted a large automated device that resembled a duster, but instead of a feathered end, it had a kind of knob covered in soft suede.

"It's a chamois for applying furniture polish. You see? You press that little lever there, just so, and ta-da!" Dimity pointed.

The chamois whirred in a rapid and rather enthusiastic manner.

The entire tea table gasped in approval.

"Oh!" said Rosie, her eyes round in awe.

Dimity looked to her. "Would you like the duster version, Rosie? The same handle apparatus comes decorated with yellow enamel flowers and a puffy lambswool duster at the end."

"Oh yes, please, ma'am!"

"I am afraid my husband needs to dance after tea, but perhaps, Lord Finbar, if you would be so kind? Mr Carefull can tell you where to purchase it."

Lord Finbar looked quite pleased to be asked to go on an errand for a parlormaid. "I would be not undelighted to provide the necessary lambswool."

"Oh, Lord Finbar, you are too kind!" Rosie jumped on her cue. Cris thought she was quite perceptive.

Lord Kirby twirled his chamois again. He looked shyly at Dimity. "It's really very fine, isn't it? I'd no idea such things existed."

"My dear Lord Kirby, there is a whole world of gadgetry awaiting you."

Cris watched this whole exchange with a kind of awed pride. His Sparkles did remarkably good work. With one wood polisher, she'd convinced Lord Finbar to leave the house in pursuit of a love token, gotten Lord Kirby interested in the modern age, and guided both vampires into chatting happily with the humans amongst them.

Even Justice was looking with interest at the exchange and the chamois. Taking stock of others rather than dwelling solely on his own tragic love story.

Dimity turned to the vampire waif next to her. "They are applying similar technology to curling tongs these days. It's really quite fantastical."

"Do go on, Mrs Carefull. I am all interest," replied the vampire.

"Well," Dimity was saying, while Cris left the room, "Your hair, of course, is perfectly lovely, but if we added a little curl to it, a touch more, simply imagine how well it would bounce as you walked down the stairs, or cast yourself into Mr Ogdon-Loppes's arms? Bouncing hair is all the rage these days. I mean to say, hair that flows is very becoming too, but bounce, I assure you, is the way of the future."

Cris left her to it. Without question, she had everything well in hand. Even the bouncing. Especially the bouncing.

CHAPTER SEVEN

The Tragedy of the Colors

And so it proved to be the case.

By the end of their first week at the Nottingham Hive, Lord Kirby had begun to carry around his automated chamois in a special holster that Justice found for him while out shopping with Dimity. Lord Kirby treated the chamois more as a kind of pet than an actual functioning tool, patting it affectionately from the sash he now wore about his robes.

Crispin made this observation to Dimity.

Dimity instantly sent Cris out about town to enquire after puppies – Corgi puppies in particular. Everyone knew Corgis were a good dog breed for the supernatural set.

By Sunday, a big-eared, short-coupled, enthusiastic Corgi puppy was suddenly in their midst. The puppy spent a good deal of time tripping everyone up as they went about their decorating tasks and leaving hair on positively everything, especially the black velvet. No doubt this was part of Dimity's intent in acquiring him – Corgis and velvet were incompatible. The little chap was so patently adorable that no one minded – they simply paused to pet him and tell him how marvelous he was. He had a tendency to stare deeply into one's eyes and then roll over given the slightest sign of affection. Lord Kirby was instantly enamored, and named the puppy *The Tragedy of the Commons*, as if he were a racing steed instead of a dog. This got rather quickly shortened to *Trudge*. Cris even saw Mr Theris sneak the puppy treats on more than one occasion.

As the house came to colorful life about them, Cris began to notice other changes Dimity had wrought as well.

Justice left off the piratical white shirts, and started wearing colorful silken robes, long skirts, and eventually, with a mix of delight and self-consciousness, a becoming blue day dress.

No one batted an eye. Vampires were known to be eccentric. In fact, Justice looked so much like a vampire queen, Cris thought (with amusement, mind you) that agents coming in fresh to Budgy Hall knowing it had vampires in residence would get mighty confused. The Nottingham Hive now apparently boasted two female vampires, and when had that ever happened? Never. Not in the history of hives.

Not that any of them had seen the actual hive queen yet. Crispin wondered if this was Dimity's secondary solution. If the baroness remained sane but refused ever to appear above ground again, Justice could simply be the de facto queen, and no one would really be the wiser.

Cris wondered if that would work.

When asked directly, Dimity said she'd consider it, and she would ask Justice how he felt about female pronouns. They left it at that for the time being. With the threat of death and BUR intervention riding on the reappearance of the baroness, that had to be the priority. Besides, BUR could be right in its extreme measures – if the queen remained below, there was a good chance the hive would slide back into Goth the moment Dimity left.

On the bright side, after a week Lord Finbar had improved considerably. He'd given over the romantics and was reading some of the more modern poets. He was also exploring transcendentalism. His jackets were still black velvet and drooping, but he'd started to branch out in the area of cravats. With Rosie's gentle encouragement, he'd been persuaded into a blood-red satin fluff. Dimity said she had high hopes that jewel tones were in his immediate future.

Cinjin Theris proved the most challenging. Despite being the recipient of playbills lauding the delights of the stages of London, he remained stubbornly in Nottingham. Dimity said she'd hoped he would leave of his own volition – finding himself on the losing end of hive control, the road to theatrical fame might seem an easier goal.

Eventually Dimity suggested that Cris try applying some pressure, Mr Theris being the type of man never to trust a woman in any way.

Cris caught the actor one evening reciting a piece of Shakespeare to the new kitchen staff. Cris was impressed despite himself. The man did have a genuine talent for the stage. Crispin spent a good hour convincing Theris that he should at least *visit* London, simply to experience some small amount of its dramaturgic wonders and expose directors to his manifold talents. Cris was as flattering as he could be to a man he abhorred.

"But my lady, the baroness! Her needs must be met," protested the drone, emphasising that he alone was responsible for delivering nibbly shepherdesses to the vampire queen.

Cris shrugged. "My wife will take care of it."

Mr Theris evaluated him. "Send you to do it, will she?"

Cris was wearing his new dancing costume. It was plain and gray, but still tight, and looked almost like the attire Arctic explorers donned under their suits for warmth.

Mr Theris curled a lip. "She'd like your looks. Except, of course, that she doesn't like any kind of change, so she might also engage in a bout of histrionics."

Cris nodded gravely. "But you need to think of your own career. She doesn't value you as an actor, clearly. Has she ever even asked you to perform for her?"

"Well, no, now that you mention it."

"You are owed your patronage dues as drone too, do you know that? Ethically and legally."

"It's not like *I* feed her." His voice was petulant. Clearly, he got the queen her shepherdesses on sufferance. Cris wondered if this was part of his obsession with controlling the hive. Had the queen stopped sucking from his neck after her retreat, thus irreparably damaging his confidence in his role as her drone and his place in the hive?

"Well there, you see? She'll be fine if you go down to visit London."

"And the others? Lord Finbar and Lord Kirby occasionally sip from me."

"Lord Finbar has Rosie now. And I believe Lord Kirby and the carpenter are coming to an arrangement. You will be missed, of course, but the hive should be fine for a short while." Cris wanted to emphasize that Theris's control over the hive was slipping, and that he had other options, without his feeling too threatened.

The arrogant fellow did seem to be considering the proposition.

Cris sweetened the pot. "It seems such a shame to deprive London of your skills. You could simply... find out."

"I suppose a few days away couldn't hurt."

Crispin went in for the kill. "I'm giving you a letter of introduction to an acquaintance of mine, Lord Akeldama. Perhaps you've heard of him?"

"Who hasn't? Nottingham isn't the ends of the earth, you know. He funds half the plays in the West End, and even an opera or two." The actor's tone was one of extreme avarice.

"So, you realize what he can do for you? He could buy your contract off this hive, either to be his drone or to put you on the stage as his new favored star."

"Interesting prospect." Theris narrowed his eyes. No doubt he knew what Crispin was trying to do – get him away from the Nottingham hive. But if the results were to his advantage, he was the kind of man to take until there was nothing left to give.

"Isn't it, though?" Crispin had reservations about Theris's character, but they were the kinds of flaws that a vampire like Lord Akeldama might enjoy taking advantage of. Plus, the drone really was a very good actor, and Lord Akeldama was also an extensive patron of the theatre, morals or no morals. It might indeed work out positively for all concerned.

Dimity could not be more pleased by her successes over the course of their first week. She was generally best at this kind of mission, but never before had she had one more exactly suited to her particular talents. She thought it might be time to approach the queen soon – setting the stage to advantage first, of course.

Really, she found herself thinking more than once, *why hasn't the War Office had me work with vampires before? Perhaps I should have taken a job with BUR from the get-go.*

Now that she had managed to lift the three hive members out of their collective doldrums, Dimity was really rather enjoying their company. Lord Kirby, in particular, was a reluctant charmer. He never smiled, of course, but there was something pleasing about the intensity of his adoration for mahogany, and something sweet about the way he glowered while shaking a finger in reprimand at Trudge. The Corgi, of course, only licked the cool finger and went about his doggie business trailing the enamoured Lord Kirby after him.

Lord Kirby even complimented Dimity on her modernizing Budgy Hall. He was the only one to notice that more gas lighting had been installed. The old metal runners in the halls had been ripped up too, the ones for the mechanicals that no longer existed. Dimity updated the flooring and then put down colorful new Persian rugs to match the wallpaper. Lord Kirby said they were lovely and soft and wouldn't Justice appreciate them under his bare feet as he wafted about?

Dimity was growing rather fond of Lord Kirby.

While Mr Theris was still around to act as escort, Dimity did her best to open a line of communication with the hive queen by sending in her human nibbles clutching Parisian fashion plates. She also began to include fabric samples. Both those to match the new dress designs offered in the plates, and the fabrics that Dimity was using to redecorate above stairs. To the samples she pinned little encouraging notes and personal thoughts. She went so far as to create her own lace Valentine's cards to act as a bastion of communication. It was, she felt, appropriate to her role as artist, too. She found a vibrant teal, about which she wrote:

> *From the brief glimpse I had of your loveliness, Baroness, this would suit your complexion beautifully. Although, of course, it can hardly do it justice.*

She sent that fabric swatch on three consecutive evenings, with her compliments every single time.

Nothing came in reply from the baroness, not even a Valentine's card, but the vampire queen was keeping all the fabric samples and fashion plates. Dimity thought that was a good sign.

Then, finally, after Sir Crispin had given him a good long talking-to, Mr Theris left for London. Dimity returned from running errands to find him and his letter of introduction gone, and the milkmaid from the first night standing forlornly on the stoop. Cris was unavailable, escorting Justice on a shopping trip and Gantry encounter. Justice had been sticking close to the hive of late, thank goodness, as it put less strain on his tether. The vampire also obviously enjoyed having Cris act as chaperon and audience to his grand *affaire d'amour du jour*.

"Oh, good evening," said Dimity to the milkmaid. "Are you up for nibble a second time? I didn't think she liked to repeat a meal. Variety being the spice of blood, and all that."

"She doesn't," said the pretty young woman. "At least, that's what I was told. But I liked her so much. She was so very gentle with me, not like one of the lads at all. And I thought, if I cleaned up really well, and wore my Sunday best, I might get a second chance. I'd be a very good snack, I would. Not try anything. Not try to stay. It's only, she seemed so unhappy, and I thought I might help with that. Cheer her up a bit."

"I think you'd best come in," said Dimity. "We need to talk."

And, after they'd had their talk, Dimity escorted Betsy (because of course that was her name) down to Baroness Ermondy. Dimity used her key (annoyed that Theris hadn't left his behind – clearly the man wanted even the hive queen to suffer in his absence), sent the young lady inside armed with fashion, and lurked about to see what might happen. She didn't go inside herself, not yet. Timing was everything with vampires – because they had so much time to work with, they respected only the best manipulation of suspense.

There was some yelling, as she'd warned Betsy there might be. But Betsy was made of stern stuff, and clearly knew what she wanted. Eventually, whatever normally happened behind the locked cave door between vampire queen and human nibble, happened.

Betsy emerged looking euphoric, and punctured, but not so pale as some of the others before her. Her neck had been wrapped in a pretty little scarf, with no blood visible, so Dimity didn't feel faint at all. And this was another good sign, that the baroness had given the girl a gift.

Betsy's grin was huge and artless. "She wants to see me again! She says I'm good in an epistemological crisis. I don't know what that means but it sounds wonderful. She says, send more fashion plates next time. She says, feed me steak and kidney pie and give me a place here because she'd like it if I were around more. Oh, and she gave me a Valentine's card of instructions to pass along as proof. I'm not sure what that means, but it sounds important."

Dimity took the card and opened it. *Carry on,* was all it said.

Dimity gave Betsy a big smile. "You, Betsy darling, are a miracle worker. Now, come along, let's get you that pie, and some steamed spinach too, I think. And I believe you ought to meet our parlormaid, Rosie. You two will get along famously."

It turned out Rosie and Betsy knew each other of old, both coming from the nearby village of Beeston. They could not have been more delighted by their reunion, if the excessive squealing that commenced was any sign.

Dimity, who dearly loved a good squeal, made them all tea in the kitchen and felt very pleased with herself.

Crispin took Justice firmly in hand – in an older brother kind of way. Odd, given the vampire was so much older than he, but Justice did so remind Cris of Tristan, he couldn't help himself.

There would be no more dramatic running through the woods – it stretched tethers too far and ruined night-rails. All trysts would be chaperoned forthwith. Cris told Justice kindly that she needed to value herself more. (Justice had decided that she preferred the feminine, when all was said and done.) Didn't Justice deserve to be courted properly? Cris thought so. Dimity added that she thought Justice should make Gantry work a little harder for her affection. Flowers, at the very least. A few nice bits of jewelry weren't to be sneezed at either!

Justice hadn't even known to request such things.

"You have all the power, young lady. Don't let him take advantage," said Cris, getting into the role and loving the way Justice glowed every time she was addressed as *young lady*. She'd never had such a thing in life, so Cris would address her correctly in afterlife. These things were important, a courtesy that took nothing from his own consequence. Dimity, of course, had impressed upon Cris that a formal and legitimate courtship would appeal more to the man's parents. If Gantry and Justice were perceived to be seriously in love and not engaged in a childish passion, drone status was a more likely outcome (once Justice's vampiric state was revealed). Still, if they dangled marriage with the wealthy ward of an eccentric baroness, surely no country gentry could refuse to permit courtship, at least?

Justice, of course, didn't want to be formal, legitimate, or sensible. She wanted a *grand passion*. Crispin was determined she should have it all.

Dimity was determined to see her in blue. Fortunately, it transpired that when the entire field of actual dresses was available to her, Justice was willing to try all colors. More than willing.

In fact, Cris had to hold her back when they went shopping. They started with only two tea dresses, four day dresses, two (additional) nightgowns, one visiting dress (because really, how often did a vampire pay calls?), two dinner dresses, and a ball gown. No, Cris did not think a promenade gown was necessary, as promenading was for sunny hours. While he devoutly believed that Justice was wonderful and could cut a swath with the best of them, going out in broad daylight was still death to a vampire.

Justice conceded this last.

Six days after placing the order, about halfway through their second week at the hive, Justice's dresses arrived.

The young vampire was incandescent with delight. They were all to the very latest standards, which meant they were tighter and narrower and beginning to lift into a bustle at the back. Dimity explained that this cut was far more suitable to Justice's small frame than the larger hoops and wider sleeves of last season.

The new gowns were also all the colors of the rainbow. One of the day dresses was even *yellow*. Justice, of course, looked stunning in all of them.

Cris made certain to tell her so as she modeled them for him and Dimity, one after another. She was still as deathly pale as could be, but now this came off as tragically lovely rather than sickly.

Dimity said with true admiration that dark-eyed brunettes had all the luck where color was concerned. "Justice, darling, I'm convinced that Gantry's parents will be delighted with you. You're a positive vision of innocent aristocratic appeal."

Crispin had worried a bit, but Justice had assured him that Gantry liked her in whatever she wore, and whatever pronouns were applied, so long as she was still Justice at heart. Crispin applauded the fellow for his adaptability, and began to think Dimity was right about Gantry. He was more than the bumbling countrified squire's son he appeared to be. And he genuinely adored Justice.

After the dresses had all been admired and discussed, Cris asked Justice (in a lovely pink ballgown) to dance. Dimity played, and Justice had the first of many lessons in how to follow on the dance floor. It was fun and amusing for all concerned.

Their deadline was looming. They'd only four more days before BUR showed up and ruined everything. Dimity probably wasn't as worried about it as she should be. In fact, she found herself dwelling more and more on the closed-door arrangement.

Sir Crispin was proving a tough nut to crack. He was remarkably stoic at bedtime, despite his obvious interest. Dimity had progressed from kissing his mouth to his neck and shoulders, and touching him most places, except where she really wanted to touch. It was simply that she wasn't sure how to do it *right*. She didn't want to hurt him at all. She knew men were delicate in that area. Of course she did, as a good deal of her training with regard to the male anatomy facilitated disabling its functionality, not improving it.

"Justice," she asked finally, late one night when she and the vampire were alone together sorting ribbons, "might I ask an indelicate question? My husband and I... That is, I have some concerns, you know, in the bedroom." She whispered the last bit.

"Oh no, dear, no, I can't join you. I'm devoted to Gantry alone, you see? Perhaps Lord Kirby..."

Dimity squeaked. "Oh no, not *that*, it's more me, I think. I'm not sure what I'm about when I'm, um, *about* his manly bits – you see?"

"Oh, my sweet summer muffin! How tragic. And I suppose you can't simply ask him, can you? Because he's like Gantry used to be, all serious and disciplined, with a stiff upper lip and a public school education."

Dimity considered. "I *could* ask him, I suppose. Does that normally work, with gentlemen?"

"In my experience, most assuredly. The only thing more delightful than the act of conjugal bliss is talking about it first. And since every man is different in his preferences, it is better to inquire after them."

Dimity blinked. "Really?"

The vampire nodded. "Absolutely. And you take my word for it, darling. I'm nearly fifty years old, don't tell. But I should know."

Dimity nodded back gravely. "Oh, Justice, I'm so glad we are friends now and that you have given up stealing my nightgowns and running though forests."

"It was only the once. But I admit, in retrospect, it was a tad extreme. I can't believe your husband witnessed it all. How embarrassing. I had no other way to run free with my dreams and passions, you see?"

Dimity did see. And what she saw was that Justice had been delighted by every aspect of that evening early on in their visit, including the fact that there had been an audience for the entire thing. Still, Dimity could be gracious in victory. "Well, I'm delighted that your dreams have turned a touch more practical and therefore more achievable."

Justice's pouty face turned tragic. "Do you think my Gantry's parents will ever come around?"

"I have an idea about that."

"I worry sometimes – *should* he become my drone? It's so confining for poor Gantry. I don't want to hold him back from his ambitions. Humans need to be free. Go to London, enjoy the clubs, marry, have children, eat garlic. That sort of thing."

Justice was being over-dramatic and ridiculous, of course. Many sought drone status – the lure of possible immortality alone was enough. But also, the patronage and the lighter workload made it a tremendously appealing career prospect. But Justice did so love an emotional wallow on occasion.

Dimity considered the scene Sir Crispin had described to her, of Gantry and Justice under the oak tree. "And he desires those things, does he? He wants to leave you? Doesn't want to stay and be yours? Doesn't adore everything about you?"

"Well..."

"Justice, darling, I believe he shares your desires, I really do. Has he ever mentioned the need for such things as marriage, children, or a steady diet of garlic?"

"Well, no, not exactly. He's always said how much he would like to be my drone. But perhaps he is only telling me what I wish to hear."

"I think you're making additional histrionic art for yourself. Has he ever lied to you before?"

"Well, noooo." Justice waved her hands about, floating and expressive, trailing the ruffles of her teal twilled silk day gown.

"There, you see? And don't worry about his parents. I shall bring them 'round."

And so, with Dimity's gentle encouragement, Gantry was at last invited to visit Budgy Hall by Lord Finbar (in lieu of the baroness).

Of course, grumpy and not sure who it was, Lord Kirby nearly had the door barred against him. Dimity sighed in frustration, acknowledging that some regressive behavior was to be expected.

"Really, Lord Kirby!" Dimity reproached him as she reopened the door. "He brought flowers. Honestly, how can you turn away any man bearing daffodils? Good afternoon, sir. You must be Mr Ogdon-Loppes? Charmed to meet you. I'm Mrs Carefull. Do come in. Your lady love and I have become great friends."

Gantry only nodded and blushed incredibly red. He already had a ruddy complexion, so this did him no favors, but he looked earnest enough. "Where is my angel?"

"She's coming down now."

Justice did love to make an entrance. So down she came, descending the stairs in a lilac muslin gown from a new Italian designer. It was trimmed in cream lace and had a scalloped hem and a modest train. The vampire positively glowed in it. She'd curled her hair, but left it loose. Even Dimity could not persuade Justice to put up her hair. "No dear, no," the vampire had explained, "it represents my free spirit. I must have it down."

Gantry gasped and let the daffodils fall from his hands, scattering yellow and bright green around his feet.

Justice floated to him.

Gantry swept the vampire up into his arms. "Oh, my own, my love, how I have missed you."

"Gantry, light of my life, you're here. Oh, you are here at last..."

Patently, Crispin had not had as much of a leavening effect as they'd hoped. Well, Rome wasn't built in a day.

"My parents, they are unmoved and unmoving," intoned Gantry.

"Oh, Gantry, you suffer so for me. How you suffer!"

The man shook his head. "They are *intellectuals*. I confuse them with my concupiscence. *We* confuse them. Our love, our dedication, they do not understand such grand passion. They are so cold and cerebral, too caught up in their stupid books!"

Dimity left them to it when they commenced an embrace in the hall that involved Justice bent back over Gantry's arm, both of them crushing daffodils underfoot. It was a good thing the new rugs were out for cleaning at the moment.

Lord Kirby said gloomily to her, "That mortal will break our little dove's heart, he will. You mark my words."

Dimity snorted at him and twiddled with the cluster brooch at her throat. "Don't be ridiculous, my dear Lord Kirby, he will do no such thing. I would never allow it. Oh, see there! Please stop Trudge, that dog will eat the daffodils. I'm convinced that can't possibly be good for him."

Lord Kirby went to rescue the puppy, who really was only snuffling at the fallen flowers, but the vampire needed a distraction.

Dimity went to write a letter to her brother. She

hadn't really wanted to deploy him. He was never very cooperative when she did. But it was becoming increasingly clear that Pillover would be necessary. And soon.

It was getting on to the end of their second week at the hive. Cris wrote to Bertie to beg for one additional week and could he convince BUR to, if not delay, at least not take drastic action right away. He emphasised that everything was going swimmingly. No doubt Dimity was also making her reports and begging for an extension. They were neither of them certain they would get any more time, so they entered a state of mutual tension. Every knock at the hive door could be a sundowner, or a team from the stabbing constabulary – or both – sent to eliminate the hive. Crispin wasn't certain what he would do under those circumstances. Would he turn traitor and warn the hive, help them to hide below with their queen? Barricade the cellar door? Would he fight for his new friends against those better trained than himself? Would Dimity? The idea of anyone killing Justice was too horrible to contemplate! Or even poor old Kirby, or grumpy old Finbar. It was unthinkable.

Obviously, he was considering fighting his own government, because his brain was coming up with battle plans. Oh, but he would give anything not to be put into the position of having to choose!

On the bright side, things were poodling along nicely now that Mr Theris was away in London. There had been no word from him or Lord Akeldama. Cris decided one of two things had happened – they'd fallen deeply in love or Akeldama had killed him on sight. Either one was an actable outcome.

Lord Finbar began making noises about enlarging and then opening up the hive's library to the public. The vampire muttered at midnight tea that the "American Emerson fellow had some very interesting stances on the education of the lower orders." This Finbar took to mean humans (as opposed to the poor). "Although it could also mean werewolves – they are, you know... lower. To the ground, at the very least. But I don't know that I could stand a pack about the place. They do smell so."

Dimity looked so pleased when he said this (about opening the library, not the pack being stinky), that Crispin knew it had all been her idea. For some reason she also insisted that Finbar read the latest Catullus translations, which she happened to have in one of her trunks. Cris wasn't sure about the reasoning behind that. Catullus could be difficult on even the most stable individuals, but Dimity had done so well so far that he wouldn't second-guess her now. There must be some good reason for foisting Catullus upon a vampire.

The company for midnight tea had grown considerably smaller over the two weeks, as most of the overhaul of Budgy Hall was now completed. It comprised Lord Finbar and his faithful Rosie. Without the hive queen above stairs, Rosie could not officially become a drone, but everyone knew she was headed in that direction. Betsy also joined them most nights. They'd subtly shifted the baroness's feeding time to after tea, so that Betsy might be well fortified for her duties. Dimity and Cris were there too, of course, and Lord Kirby and at least one of the lingering tradesfolk. Lord Kirby kept finding more things for them to do, especially the carpenter. Finally, Justice made up the last of the party, and Gantry too, most evenings now. Lord Kirby had stopped glaring at him when it became clear that Gantry adored dogs, and Trudge in particular. Gantry kept calling the Corgi his *short-coupled little chap* in tones of great affection, and wondering if he might take him hunting sometime. "I'll wager you could find me a downed pheasant, couldn't you? There's a good hound!"

Cris would never accuse the assembly of being *cheerful* or even *pleasant*. Finbar still waffled on about poetry, and Kirby still frowned at everything and everyone, and Justice and Gantry still made limpid eyes at each other and waxed purple in prose. But it was certainly more tolerable than it had been initially, and really, what more could you ask of a vampire hive than *tolerable*?

Budgy Hall was spectacular (at least its receiving rooms). Dimity not only embraced color – it turned out she had excellent taste and a good eye to go with it. While her own personal preferences in attire could best be described as *ostentatious*, she'd managed elegance with the hive house. It was still showy, but she stuck to deep jewel tones and metallics throughout, with cream as a unifying counter-color. In the end this resulted in a harmonious series of rooms that might grace any grand house in London, even that of Lord Akeldama himself (although with fewer naked cherubs). Cris had never visited Lord Akeldama, but everyone knew about the cherubs.

Cris was extremely impressed with Dimity's results and he told her so.

"Why, didn't you know, darling? I'm very, very good at my job."

She was getting more daring with him too. And he was having a rather difficult time holding out against her at bedtime. He was also beginning to forget why he kept trying.

For one thing, she took it as settled that he would brush out her hair every night. He'd taken it on as a sacred duty and mild torture. Nothing could be more sensual than sliding the bristles through and touching the soft mass of her honey curls, the scent of lemon wafting up. The sensation in his fingertips as they caressed the smooth skin of her cheeks and neck was almost euphoric.

Despite the hair brushing, he'd been doing well at resisting, and then she switched tactics and began asking him questions while they prepared for bed. Rather explicit questions.

"I was talking with Justice earlier."

"Were you indeed? Is there a shawl in a new shade of blue that needs acquiring?"

"Don't be mean. Justice in blue has changed everything! Gantry is properly courting her now."

"Yes, indeed. So, no shawls, then?"

"No. Sex. We were talking about sex."

Cris stopped brushing her hair in shock. What a very crude word. "We were? I thought we were talking about shawls."

Her shoulders were tense. "Not *us*. Justice and I were discussing carnal relations. You see, I was trying to inquire after doing it properly, since you obviously won't start the thing up and therefore I must, but I'm not sure quite how to go about it. So then I thought, what ho! I've a new vampire friend to call upon. After all, Justice has decades of experience and seems inclined to play various possible roles in the bedroom and therefore she should know all about what's what."

"Uh," said Cris, lost, feeling hot about the ears and aroused by interest and embarrassment. He resumed brushing.

She turned and took the brush away from him, putting it on a chair next to her side of the bed. She was crimson-faced, but she also had that glint in her eyes that suggested this was a matter as serious as the right color brocade cushion, and she would *not* be gainsaid.

She took a deep breath and then spoke fast and all at once, practically without pause. "Here's what I don't know. How should you like to be touched, you know, down there? Hard or soft? Is it like a cooked sausage or an uncooked one? Do I hold firm like a cricket bat, or am I gentle, like a cat's tail? Do I tug, or swirl about? Is it up and down or side to side or sort of squeezing? I suspect what I need is some kind of primary instruction manual or guidebook – you know, like we get before a mission in a foreign city. Would you write one up for me? Would that work? I want you to be comfortable."

Cris couldn't help it, she was so earnest, and so eager, and so sweet.

"Oh, Sparkles, you've been giving this a not inconsiderable amount of thought, haven't you?"

"For a very, *very* long time. One only really learns by doing, of course, but you've taken ages to come around to me, Sir Crispin. I don't want to mess it all up now that I've finally caught your interest."

"Silly Sparkles, you've always had my interest."

"You frown because you love me?"

"Exactly."

"So?"

"Cooked sausage, up and down, halfway between cat's tail and cricket bat. With something to make it smooth, like oil or face cream."

"Face cream? Really? No one has ever mentioned face cream. If I were very good and went slowly, would you let me touch?"

Cris officially gave up at that juncture. Raised the white flag of surrender and everything. Well, raised something, that's certain. He was trying to protect his own virtue when clearly, he hadn't any. How was he expected to hold out, and why was he bothering to keep doing so?

He was going to marry this woman anyway – she'd already pronounced it. And, as far as he was concerned, it would happen as soon as he could rustle up the necessary paperwork. All those contacts he'd cultivated over his years in the War Office were about to come in very handy indeed.

He might as well let her have at.

So he stripped down entirely, not embarrassed at all, because he'd been cavorting about in bathing costumes for a fortnight anyway, so she knew all. In fact, practically all of Nottingham had seen practically all of Sir Crispin, so who was he to mind full nudity?

Dimity's eyes were wide and awed and covetous. "Ooooh, you have hair in strange places."

He lay back, put his hands behind his head on the pillow, and looked up at her. He took a moment to be pleased the chimneys were now clean and they had a cheerful fire in the grate. He did want to put on a good showing.

"You know," said Dimity, as if she were realizing it and saying it at the same time, which was rarely a safe tactic, "the only time you're ever still is like this, alone with me."

"You're the only thing I've ever wanted to stop moving for."

"Oh. Goodness. Look at you." Her gaze was hungry and running all over him. He'd never had anyone look at him like this before – as if he were entirely worthy and wanted, as if he were needed and necessary.

He thought he would simply lie there and she would be shy and retiring and cautiously tentative and they'd see where things went. Her touch would likely be too light and do no more than tickle. She probably would not even think to use her mouth and she'd have to be gently coaxed into everything.

He was entirely wrong about all of it.

Afterwards, when they lay hot and sticky and panting, he realized his Sparkles had magic hands and he hoped she'd surmised that her tuppenny knight had a magic tongue.

"There's more, isn't there?" Her body was supine,

gracefully curved by relaxation. Her eyes were big and bright and glorious.

"Mmm," he replied, feeling weighted into bonelessness and heavy-lidded.

She rolled over him and drew lazy patterns in the spend lying white and sticky on his abdomen. Not at all squeamish, it turned out, his lady love. He was incredibly grateful to discover that blood was the only bodily fluid that made her faint.

"I want to try all of it," she said, sucking a finger and making an interested face.

"Mmm," he said, only dozing off a little.

"Don't fall asleep yet. This is serious."

The sun was up and the new curtains kept most of it out, but he could still see the rose flush on her skin. She was smooth all over, it turned out, and perfectly shaped, all softly curved, exactly as he'd always imagined. Honey-colored curls. Honey-flavored skin. Honey-flavored everything.

He licked his lips and felt himself stir again. "I'm listening."

"It'll be us now, I've decided. This is us now. We're not going back to the way it was before, when you thought you should resist me. And Justice can have all my nightgowns, even the new ones."

"Marvelous idea."

"And even when we're done here, sometimes you'll wear a dancing costume only for me."

"Just for you." His sleep contentment turned to utter pleasure, to be so completely wanted. What more could he possibly need?

"Even the striped one, because I know you don't

like it, but it's very tight and the white stripes are sort of see-through in places and—"

"Yes, Sparkles, even the stripy one."

"And we can do more of this tomorrow? I want to try licking you all over until you spend in my mouth. And I want to, you know, go riding... the fun way."

"Both in one night?" he squeaked, opening his eyes in surprise.

"Is that not possible? You see, I have much to learn."

He grumbled at her something about his needing to learn things too, since she made the best noises he'd ever heard while in the throes of pleasure and he wanted to collect them all, over and over again.

"Promise?" she said, a whisper of longing tickling his chest hair.

"Promise," he replied.

And he wasn't sure what it was he'd just promised her, but it didn't really matter, because he would give it to her anyway, whatever she wanted.

CHAPTER EIGHT

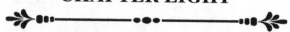

The Vampires Are Convinced to Throw a Party, Despite Themselves

Dimity was beginning to feel guilty.

She was hiding from Cris the fact that she had taken to escorting Betsy down to her trysts with the hive queen. She didn't think she was in any danger. She never spent any time with the bally red-headed fang-toothed snoot. Dimity was rarely even in danger of fainting, as Betsy often emerged with no punctures at all and only love bites to show for her encounter. This was a sign of great improvement in the baroness's mental state. For it meant that she was eating only when she needed sustenance, and not to prove some kind of medieval point.

But Dimity knew Sir Crispin, as her safety, wouldn't like that she went down into the cave essentially unprotected. And now he, as her lover, wouldn't like it that she was placing herself in a position to be corrupted. Because everyone knew it was nigh on impossible to resist the lure of a vampire queen. On the bright side, wasn't *lover* a delightful word? Dimity wanted to write missives to all her friends immediately: Sidheag in the North, Sophronia gallivanting about the Continent, and Agatha who was... well, who knew where Agatha was? But Dimity wanted to write to them all anyway, simply to crow: "Guess what has happened to me? I have taken a *lover!*" Then she would add something on how very peculiar was the way that men functioned physically, in matters carnal – enthusiastic and vulnerable and messy. Who knew? Certainly not Dimity. Now, of course, she was delighted by her discovery, and she was bound and determined to see if she could completely master one specific part of Sir Crispin's anatomy. With the expectation, of course, that said anatomy could obey her over him and his legendary control, for always. It was a point of *pride*.

But of course, one didn't write those sorts of letters. Not even to one's true friends.

Still, other things were coming along enthusiastically too (not just Sir Crispin's nether regions).

She'd been working on Lord Finbar, for example, with excellent results. The library was now being expanded – Lord Kirby's carpenter friend was back. Lord Finbar expressed profound admiration of the Catullus translation Dimity had given him, and continued interest in the works of the transcendentalists. This could only be considered progress.

It might be going too well, in fact, because he asked her one night, with dour timidity, if he might practice an oratory endeavor upon her.

"Practice, Lord Finbar?"

"Well, I have been giving considerable thought to

your idea of an intellectual salon, Mrs Carefull, perhaps a small gathering of high-minded, respectably grave individuals."

"My suggestion? Surely that was your idea, dear Lord Finbar?"

"Was it? How perspicacious of me. Well then, it should most certainly happen."

"I couldn't agree more. Shall I send out invitations?" Dimity had, of course, already prepared them all.

"Oh, would you? That would be very kind, indeed. I'm sure you know who best to invite." As if Dimity had lived in Nottingham all her life instead of merely two weeks.

She stood to leave.

"No, no, my dear Mrs Carefull, please remain a moment longer. If I could simply practice with you? Of course one should not be so nervous, but..."

"Oh, but wouldn't Rosie be a better choice of audience?"

"Rosie is a lovely girl, but not particularly cerebral. I believe that you are better equipped to understand the somber quality and melancholic nuances of my work."

Dimity, after a moment's consideration, decided it would be better to have this over and done with sooner rather than later. "Very well, sir. I'm all ears."

Lord Finbar began, and Dimity realized he was not so far along as she had hoped. He clearly needed a great deal more work. And it was, perhaps, beyond the purview of even her not inconsiderable talents to eliminate Byron when he had taken root so firmly.

I stand alone at the edge of the abyss.
Remembering.
Oh, remembering.
That you are only beautiful when you cry.
No, oh no.
Do not take your love away, in deathly song.
All is winter in my heart.
I pray you murder me, like eggs falling over the
cliff of forever.
For now, all I see is darkness and destruction.
The angels are dead.
I need nothing. I am nothing.
Sadness rains.

Dimity began to clap.

"Oh, but that is only the first verse, Mrs Carefull."

"Oh, dear me! I was overwhelmed by the profound nature and depth of feeling in your beautiful words."

"Shall I go on, then?"

"Oh, dear sir, but I don't think I could bear it. Too powerful, too moving." She squeezed out a few tears. Dimity had always excelled at crying on cue.

Lord Finbar watched the perfect crystalline drops trickle down her cheek in awe. Dimity did not wipe them away – why should she? They weren't that easy to produce!

"Oh, you poor, delicate, sentimental young jewel. I've done you in, haven't I?"

"Oh, sir, it is a tremendous talent you possess. How did it survive your metamorphosis? One would think you still human, with such depth of meaning in your stanzas. How could you not present to a broader audience? An intellectual salon is exactly the thing. We simply must invite others to listen to your greatness and be similarly moved by it."

"You don't think I would be showing up the other speakers, do you? One wishes to be welcoming to all levels and abilities. It's not putting myself too far forward – a poem of such grave magnitude?"

"Well, perhaps only one verse at a time? Over a series of assemblies? All at once might be a touch overwhelming for weaker human constitutions. Lives might be lost."

"My dear Mrs Carefull, how thoughtful you are. I shall take this under advisement. Of course, my melancholy might detrimentally affect others. It's quite deep, you see? One does not wish to drag any poor, unsuspecting humans into the depressive depths that hold a man such as myself in their yearning maw."

Dimity patted his hand. "I understand perfectly. You merely wish us to experience your pain, share it a little, but not dwell in the darkness with you."

"Exactly so."

"Then indeed, I urge all caution in your oratory pursuits, dear Lord Finbar. The damage you could do with any more than a single verse could be profound and have wide-ranging repercussions."

He nodded gravely. "I understand. Poetry can be too powerful."

"And thus others must be eased into it. Your library idea is a wonderful prospect. After all, these days most young ones are taught to read, so eventually they too may enjoy poetry. And your oration will most certainly inspire them."

"You are too kind, Mrs Carefull. Too kind."

"Now, Lord Finbar. Have you considered, for this debut of your salon, a new jacket perhaps? Something emerald green? I do so think you need a *signature* color. All the great poets had a signature color. And black is so over-worn in poetry circles, don't you feel?"

"Green, you think, Mrs Carefull?"

"Emerald green, Lord Finbar. It will bring out your eyes." Which was a belter of a lie, as his eyes were so sunken she had no idea what color they were.

"Do you think little Miss Rosie would like me in emerald green, Mrs Carefull?"

"Most assuredly, Lord Finbar. Most assuredly." With which she beat a hasty retreat, as he looked inclined to begin another verse.

Accordingly, invitations to an *Intellectual Salon at Budgy Hall* were delivered and the replies came back with alacrity. It seemed Nottingham wanted nothing more than a new cerebral gathering of pedants in its midst. The fact that it was being hosted by a vampire hive was, of course, left off the invitations. But eccentric aristocrats reciting poetry were deemed, even in the very best of drawing rooms, to be almost as worthy.

If the Ogdon-Loppeses knew the truth behind Budgy Hall or connected the salon to their youngest son's inappropriate love affair, they made no objection. For they were the first to accept.

Unfortunately, all was not entirely smooth sailing for Dimity and Sir Crispin.

Cris was horrified to open the door just before sunrise, with everyone preparing for bed, to find Mr Theris smirking on the stoop. He had with him a large man, well-dressed but scruffy, with a certain commanding glint to his eye. Crispin had never served with Lord Maccon of the Woolsey Pack, but he'd had the Alpha pointed out to him in the ranks. The head of BUR had a reputation for being gruff and exacting, occasionally brutal, and generally fair. Because Cris worked for the War Office, he also knew what authority the werewolf standing before him in greatcoat and top hat carried for the Crown – he was a sanctioned sundowner. He was allowed, legally and without trial, to kill other supernatural creatures.

Greetings exchanged and introductions made, Lord Maccon gave Cris such a knowing look it was clear he was aware of their infiltration operation.

Lord Maccon made a weak excuse for the actor's benefit. "Your pardon for arriving unannounced. Mr Theris kindly said he'd escort me to see Budgy Hall. I've an interest in architecture and it is an excellent example of its type."

"Oh, indeed, what type is that?" asked Cris.

"Oh, erm, architectural." The werewolf shrugged and looked a bit confused. Clearly, he was not one for conducting infiltrations himself. Crispin might have made it easier on the man, but Cris was nervous and flummoxed to find the biggest threat to the hive's survival simply standing there on the landing.

"Indeed so, Lord Maccon. As you say." Cris did not invite him in. He wanted to. For surely Dimity's makeover would impress even the most hardened of sundowners. Or Scottish lords. But he couldn't. One didn't invite a werewolf into a vampire hive without a great deal of pomp and circumstance and clearance first. Even vampires as absent-minded as Justice, Kirby, and Finbar would know a werewolf when they smelled one. And without their queen to stabilize them and their emotional reactions to the unexpected presence of another predator in their house? Who knew how they might react?

Fortunately, it seemed Lord Maccon knew all of this and was merely on their stoop to make Dimity aware that he was in town. For now.

Lord Maccon pretended to look at the night sky. "Time is running out." The implication was that he meant sunrise, and it was for Theris's benefit. Crispin knew that he really meant saving the queen. Theris barely noticed. He was occupied in kicking at the stoop impatiently while the niceties were exchanged.

Lord Maccon tilted his hat and turned to go.

"Wait just a moment, my lord?" Crispin reached behind to the entryway table for one of the extra invitations. Dimity had made them up on thick card stock with lace detail and gilt, very ornate and impressive (and almost Valentine-like). "An intellectual salon, my lord. A few evenings from now. Let us prove our mettle, sir. You won't be disappointed."

Lord Maccon took the invitation and tapped the corner of the envelope against his teeth. "I'll be made welcome?"

"Of course, sir." Dimity's persuasive abilities were about to be truly tested, but what better way to show off how far the hive had come than by proving they could tolerate a werewolf in their midst without flinching, and recite poetry at the same time?

"A gathering, here?" No doubt Lord Maccon had been told the hive was in full retreat and going to Goth. The fact that there was a party in the works could only be seen as a good sign.

"Here, sir."

The big werewolf nodded. "We shall see if it's good enough. A respite, then, until the party." With which he swept away, greatcoat trailing in his wake as he strode down the cobbled street at an impressive clip. Crispin caught a glance, as the coat flapped, of the gun holstered at his hip. A small, fat revolver with a square grip – a Galand Tue Tue. Crispin knew his munitions. He'd once been in charge of them for his regiment. The Tue Tue was one he knew of but had never seen outside of schematics, for it had been designed with only one purpose – to kill vampires.

Mr Theris finally spoke, revealing that he didn't know Lord Maccon was a supernatural creature and could still hear him. "Cad. Who is he to judge us? Bally Scotsman got himself a title and fancy digs in London. We met on the train up. First class will let anyone in these days."

Crispin blinked at him, startled. This proved a remarkable lack of social acumen, even for Mr Theris. The story of Lord Maccon's becoming Alpha to the Woolsey Pack was common knowledge in London society. Even if the fact that he was licensed to kill supernatural creatures wasn't.

Judiciously, Crispin said, "He would be an

excellent addition to our upcoming gathering, regardless."

"Oh, indeed? And what gathering is that?" Mr Theris stepped in, tossing his top hat at the stand and missing it, so that one of the new maids had to run after and pick it up.

"Lord Finbar is hosting an intellectual salon and literary gathering."

"Bloody hell," said Mr Theris, succinctly.

Cris carefully did not invite the actor to participate. The man lacked all class – he'd probably choose to recite *Hamlet*. "How was your trip to London? Did the stage embrace you? Did Lord Akeldama?"

Mr Theris wrinkled his nose and handed over a missive, seal unbroken. This surprised Cris. He hadn't thought Mr Theris capable of that kind of discretion. Cris cracked it and read the vampire's neat firm hand with interest. Various words were underlined for emphasis:

> *No, Sir Crispin, no. He is not for me and I am, most assuredly, not for him. I do have an idea, however. If this fellow is a bit much, even to become one of my droney-poos, without question Nottingham cannot hope to cope with him long term. Let the werewolves have him, dear boy. Werewolves are always up for the hardest and messiest of jobs.*

Cris looked up. "Are you sure Lord Maccon is that much of a bounder, Mr Theris? One would think you had a few things in common."

"Bit of a brute, truth to tell."

"Exactly what I meant."

Mr Theris paused, clearly unsure whether he'd been insulted or not. "Well, erm, quite. And how are things here in poor old Notts?"

Cris gestured wide to indicate the transformed hive house, practically glowing with vibrancy and decorative aplomb.

Mr Theris managed to look both impressed and discomfited. Of course he went on the attack. "And how has your wife been rubbing along with the baroness?"

"My wife?"

"Oh yes, didn't you know? She's been taking the human nibbles down to the queen every night in my place. I passed along the responsibility to her. Or I did when I left."

"She *WHAT*?" Crispin's stomach dropped into his knees. His knees were not ready for that and began to shake.

"Oh yes. None of us thought Baroness Ermondy would put up with that nonsense, but presumably she has, or I'd already have heard the screaming rants. Used to be that if any of us tried to change anything around the hive, or even recommended a change, the baroness had hysterics. After she had her last big fit and took to her cave, all the other drones left."

"They *left*, did they?" Cris tried to calm himself, still upset that Dimity had apparently been seeing the queen, or at least seeing the queen was fed, *by herself* most nights. They were going to have a nice long conversation about that!

"Yes, they left, *en masse*, so to speak."

"So you say." Cris genuinely wondered if Mr Theris didn't think he'd hounded them out, or if he was that good an actor.

Suddenly, Mr Theris snorted, muscled his way into the front parlor, and put down his suitcase. "Let us be perfectly frank with one another, Mr Carefull. Performer to performer."

"Must we, Mr Theris?"

"You two are no more interested in becoming drones to this hive than you are married to each other."

"Is that what you think, Mr Theris?"

"That's what I think." He was back to looking smug. "London didn't go well, I take it?"

"What makes you say that?"

"We had all hoped you would stay, take to the stage where you evidently belong."

"I'm sure you did. Now what did that woman of yours do to my room while I was away?"

"Whatever it was, I'm sure it's a vast improvement."

"I don't know what you two are really about, Mr Carefull, but now that I'm back, I intend to stop you."

"Too late, Mr Theris, far too late. There's an intellectual salon imminent."

The next night, after waking, everyone made a show of being pleased to see Mr Theris returned. Dimity more than anyone. It seemed no one was *actually* pleased to see him, however. Dimity sighed. One more problem to solve. Not to mention the fact that, as Crispin had told her before they went to sleep, BUR's chief sundowner was in town – armed. Never, she thought, had there been more pressure put on the success of an event then there was on Lord Finbar's wet-blanket efforts at an intellectual salon. *Oh dear.*

Mr Theris kept turning up as she made the rounds, checking in on all her final projects. She caught him chatting with Lord Finbar in the library, apparently disgusted by the expansion in progress, the new shelves and comfortable chairs. The actor was blatantly dismissive of poor Rosie, who was in tears in one corner. Lord Finbar was throwing her distressed little looks while Mr Theris gesticulated widely and complained about *excess*, and *why on earth did the impoverished need to read, for goodness' sake*? Apparently, Lord Finbar had shocked Theris with the hive's intent to establish a lending library for the benefit of the underprivileged.

Dimity rushed to Rosie, tutted at Lord Finbar, ignored Mr Theris, and guided the distressed girl away for tea.

Later that same night, she found Mr Theris flirting outrageously with the kindly middle-aged carpenter while poor Lord Kirby slouched in a corner of the parlor looking morose and miserable. Even Trudge seemed disgruntled. Sitting at Lord Kirby's feet, the Corgi looked up with worried dark eyes at the vampire, one paw on top of the vampire's shoe. Really, Mr Theris was too bad! Too much, too domineering. It seemed, with the queen gone, he'd stepped into the void and the vampires, lost, had let him. Well, Dimity would not allow it to occur again!

Dimity told Lord Kirby that she needed his help post haste and took him away.

Lord Kirby didn't want to go, but Dimity only whispered, "Betsy will be here soon. Betsy can take on Mr Theris and win."

Betsy was no milkwater miss. She adored the queen, and she'd taken over Mr Theris's proper role of main drone and human nibble without flinching, and with a great deal more grace and aplomb. After all, he had neglected even to feed Baroness Ermondy himself! She would take on Mr Theris with all the righteous indignation of the newly responsible.

Also, Dimity had long since shown Betsy how to use a muff pistol.

Dimity took Lord Finbar to Lord Kirby in the library. She hadn't wanted to be so direct with this particular arrangement, but the unexpected return of Mr Theris was mucking up her schedule.

"How are the plans coming along for the salon on Thursday, Lord Finbar?"

"As well as one might expect, Mrs Carefull." Which was Lord Finbar's way of saying everything was going swimmingly.

"I've been meaning to ask you something for a long time, Lord Finbar. With all your attention on these new enterprises, opening the library to the public and hosting the salons, both of which I have no doubt will be wildly successful – not to mention your wonderful poetry – are you not a little overwhelmed in your praetoriani duties as well?"

Lord Kirby, behind her, gasped. "Mrs Carefull, what are you doing?"

"Hush now, let me continue. Lord Finbar, are you not feeling a tad stretched? I don't want you to overtax yourself. Plus, you have Rosie now to think of."

Lord Finbar nodded. "Yes, of course, Rosie. How is the lass? Mr Theris was rather unkind to her, I'm afraid. I forgot about him, of course. Was away somewhere for a spell. Not sure where he's been. Overtaxed, you think? Yes, it is rather a lot for me to take on alone, and one has the depths of one's melancholy to consider. One wouldn't want to take on so much that one loses touch with one's wallowing in melancholic depths, would one? Don't you feel similarly, Mrs Carefull?"

"Of course I do. So you see my point, dear sir? Lord Kirby has the perfect solution."

"Does he indeed? And what's that, old chum?" Finbar looked with interest at his fellow hive member.

Lord Kirby worried the end of his sleeve tassel, looking at Dimity imploringly. He'd taken to shorter robes over trousers, with narrower sleeves and longer tassels, in lighter colors. Presumably to help control the appearance of Corgi hairs everywhere. But Dimity felt certain the velvet would not last much longer. When it came to a competition between dog hair and velvet, the dog hair always won.

"He was telling me only last night – it was last night, wasn't it, Lord Kirby? Anyway, he was telling me he worried for you, Lord Finbar. He worries you do too much."

"Oh, Kirby, my dear fellow, too kind." Finbar

looked near to tears.

"And I was saying, he might have to sacrifice, you see, to help you out, for the good of the hive. And your melancholy, of course."

"Oh, surely not!"

"As you were saying, Lord Finbar, you need time to wallow."

"Yes, I was saying that recently, wasn't I?"

"So we were thinking, Lord Kirby and I, perhaps praetoriani is too much for you? Perhaps it's time to slough off the coils of hive concerns and the safeguarding of the queen. Lord Kirby is ready. Ready and willing."

"Oh, is he? It's not too much for you, old man? It's such a burden, I wouldn't want to curse you so."

Lord Kirby started and blinked at Dimity, but he wasn't so far gone as to not follow her crafty machinations towards his greatest wish. "Oh no, old chap, I assure you! I mean to say, of course it's a terrible burden, terrible. But anything to help the hive, my dear fellow. Anything."

"There, you see?" said Dimity.

"Are you sure?" Lord Finbar looked almost pleased.

Lord Kirby was very grave. "Indubitably."

"Our queen will have to approve the switch, of course, should she ever come out. But I think it's a capital idea. Allows me to pursue my new projects and have time to wallow. You always cared more for her safety and hive management than I did, anyway. Never knew why she had to foist the bally position on me."

"That's settled, then?" Dimity slapped her hands

together and rubbed them. "Topping. Now, shall we discuss Mr Theris? I'm not quite certain what to do about him. I was wondering if he can be trusted to attend our little gathering of like minds, or if he needs some task to keep him out of the house, or if you might consider relaxing our standards a touch and allowing one of the local werewolves to visit? Courting, if you would. When I think of Mr Theris, I think *claviger*. Don't you?"

"Werewolves! Werewolves." Lord Kirby's lip curled. "Ruffians! Scoundrels! Scandalmongers! The lot of them."

Lord Finbar added, "They aren't very intellectual."

Dimity nodded. "Perhaps only one claviger and one werewolf, then? A very special werewolf, all the way from London."

"But why, Mrs Carefull? Whyever involve them?"

"Well, you see, I have this idea..."

They quarreled that night. A real quarrel, not a sham one to push the hive in a new decorative direction or to showcase the efficiency of a good noise-muffling tapestry. He'd been stewing over it too, since Mr Theris had let loose the goose the night before.

It was because Sparkles had been attending the hive queen alone with only Betsy for company. Cris thought it was a perfectly reasonable thing to quarrel about, his being her safety and all.

"We still don't know if she's sane or not," was his point.

"She's actually being very tame with Betsy. She's not gorging herself anymore. She lets me catch glimpses of her from the doorway. Betsy says she talks sweet."

"Stomach talk, Sparkles. You know how mellow and chatty people get after a nice meal."

"Well yes, but—"

"It's such a big risk. At least let me go down with you."

"No, that'll scare her. I know it will. A strange man, even one as pretty as you? It has to be me, or Betsy, or Mr Theris."

"Never again, not that man. He shouldn't be allowed near her. Probably filling her head with nonsense, plus his blood can't be healthy for her. It's probably full of strange humors."

"Yes, I agree. Please, Cris, let me do this my way? I still have my pistol with me."

"Oh, and that has sundowner bullets in it, does it?"

"Well, no."

"Sparkles! We have someone in town to handle this!"

"He won't give her a fighting chance. I know he won't. It has to be me." It was the tone of voice she got before she stripped him bare and pounced. The one that said she would not be stymied by anything or anyone.

He had to trust her.

But his trust was tested even further as for the two nights leading up to the salon, Dimity dressed in a low-necked ballgown, a recently ordered one too – tightly fitted and puffy only at the back. This, Cris had learned to his great disappointment, was a bustle.

He wasn't sure what she was about, why she had to dress up. Or why she had to show as much neck as a human nibble might.

But both nights she vanished into the limestone caves and came back to him unscathed.

There was something desperate to their lovemaking on the evenings following. Because Cris hadn't liked that she felt the need to keep a secret from him. And Dimity clearly felt she must reassure him of her trust.

He realized that he'd told her, not so very long ago, that she was both things. She was his Sparkles and she was the Honey Bee. But somehow he'd forgotten. He'd let himself fall in love with *Dimity*, forgetting that the Honey Bee took risks. The Honey Bee had to take risks. It was her job.

And there was always the possibility that he would lose Dimity because of the Honey Bee's responsibilities.

Dimity didn't know that sex could become both comfort and reassurance. She certainly had never thought she'd be the one doing the comforting. She'd assumed, when they entered this new state of carnal bliss, that Cris would remain her safety. She was beginning to realize that sometimes she would need to be his.

There was something lost about him, after they quarreled. She was desperate to find him again. It wasn't that she hadn't trusted him, only that she'd known he wouldn't like her visiting the queen alone, and she'd been trying to protect him, in her way.

They both knew she was right. They both knew it was her job.

But like finding her with a pistol pointed at Mr Theris, the danger inherent in a vampire queen scared him. Cris was afraid for her, and that was a hundred times worse than being afraid for himself. So Dimity tried to show him she was well, she was whole, and she was his in any way she could be.

Not that he remained passive under her. He always let her explore, always let her do whatever she wished to him and his body at the start, but he never lasted all that long without paying her back.

Her Cris, her man, was never truly still, and he was like that in bed as well. Always having to do and to please, looking after her, making certain she was happy, several times, before he allowed himself his own release. Before he allowed her to win. Because it was *winning*, so far as Dimity was concerned.

She'd already learned so many things in so few nights. She'd learned what she enjoyed, and what else she maybe wanted to try, not to mention a few things that probably wouldn't be her favorites.

Honestly, even though she suspected the position was considered rather banal, she liked him over her best. The weight of him. She liked to wrap her arms and legs around his hard, lean body, squeezing as tight as she could. She liked the way her limbs looked coiled around him. For he was tan all over, so it wasn't only his outdoor activities that turned him brown. (Unless, of course, he was prone to doing those activities naked.)

She liked rubbing against him, her nipples in his chest hair, and she liked the gradual way he sank into her, always slow and always careful and always, always kind. And she liked the way, if she held him close enough and tight enough for long enough, he sometimes forgot to be careful, but he never forgot to be kind.

CHAPTER NINE

On the Transcendent Nature of
Interpretive Dance

"Oh, Lord Finbar? Lord Finbar? Oh, there you are!"

The vampire was in the library putting the finishing touches to his arrangements.

The library was near twice the size as previous. As its collection was not yet sufficient to fill all the shelves, it was currently characterized by a certain sparseness, but it would be marvelous, Dimity knew, in only a few years.

It was a true library, however, for only in this one room had Dimity permitted the Gothic aesthetic to survive. All the furniture was dark and heavy, but also plush and welcoming. She'd chosen gold brocades and brown leather, not black. It had the general feel of a gentleman's club or a very nice cigar box, and it was easy to see why Lord Finbar loved it so very much. Dimity had replaced the old worn carpet with a subdued affair of maple-leaf paisley, and added a large bay window seat to the back – with thick, heavy wine-red curtains to keep the sun out, seeing as both vampires and books need protection.

In front of those curtains, Lord Finbar had arranged a little stage upon which rested one ornately fabulous gilt chair – for the featured orators. Facing this stage, he'd brought in and set up the dining chairs, with all the other settees and wing-back chairs of the library turned about to face the stage from their various nooks.

"My, but it looks very fine, Lord Finbar. Perfectly melancholy, yet attentive."

"You're too kind, Mrs Carefull. Ah, are these the first of our guests?"

"No indeed, Lord Finbar, these are two of our presenters. Please allow me to introduce my dearest brother to you. You have read his excellent translation of Catullus, I believe."

"Your brother? The noted Latin translator? Here? In my hive! What an honor. Welcome, sir, welcome indeed." If it were possible for Lord Finbar to look pleased, then he no doubt would.

Dimity's brother, Pillover, was an Oxford don who did very little in life but mutter about things in Latin and overindulge in the pudding course. Dimity considered him, of course, an utterly useless codswallop, always had, but for some reason the intellectual set absolutely adored him. He was also, she hated to admit, the better looking of the two of them. Dimity knew herself to be passing pretty, and she'd been trained to make the most of her assets, but Pillover was a sulky, pouty slob who looked like some dark fallen angel with transcendent thoughts and secret passions.

He was no such thing, of course, but tell that to the young ladies always setting their caps at him.

"Oh, please do calm yourself, Lord Finbar. He's not a drone candidate, you understand? Yes, I told him what you are and that this is a hive house. You may depend upon his discretion – he doesn't gossip. In fact, he has very little to do with the modern world."

"I prefer the past," intoned Pillover, "and the supernatural set is of little consequence to me." He nodded at the vampire and looked around the library with interest.

Dimity continued her explanation-meets-character-assassination-of-her-brother with glee. "As you can see, he is impossibly glum and dour, so I believe you two will get along famously. And this is his friend and colleague, Professor Fausse-Maigre. And now, I really must leave you. I have to make certain Cook is ready in the kitchen. She should open the port now, I think, to let it breathe. And I was thinking perhaps whiskey as well? Isn't whiskey a terribly important thing for authors?"

"It is in my circles," said Pillover with a grunt of approval.

Dimity rolled her eyes at him and dashed off.

"Your sister is—" She heard Professor Fausse-Maigre start to say.

Pillover interrupted before his friend could finish the thought. "Yes, I *know*."

Cris drifted through the house and the party preparations and tried to be of use wherever he might. He ran into Dimity only once, as she bustled enthusiastically about. Her hazel eyes were practically incandescent with delight. She was clearly having a fantastic time of it – ordering everyone around.

She asked if he might consider an interpretive dance as part of the evening's entertainment. In the background? During Professor Fausse-Maigre's presentation on higher common sense?

Cris said he wasn't sure they had the space, and really, how did one balletically represent higher common sense?

Dimity merely hustled him into the library to talk to said professor on the matter and then trotted off again, leaving him surrounded by lilting academics who'd apparently started in on the whiskey early. Cris was reminded of one of Bertie's sayings: *Never leave an open bottle near a clergyman, a writer, or an academic. Not if you want it back again.*

Professor Fausse-Maigre explained he usually had a slate board and chalk for this speech, but lacking a visual assist, a man in a bathing costume cavorting on a small stage behind him could only add to the greater intellectual acumen of the assembly.

This sounded nonsensical to Cris, but since he wished to make the evening as much a success as possible, he allowed himself to be convinced to change into his dancing attire. He put on the gray costume, not the striped one, because he remembered what Dimity had said about half the stripes being see-through. And really, no one needed *that* much common sense *thrust* upon them.

Lord Finbar was puttering about, morose yet

happy, Rosie at his elbow, helping to fetch and carry and generally making herself useful. Dimity's brother appeared from some corner of the library where he'd been distracted by obscure Latin of interest. He didn't introduce himself, simply gave Cris the raised eyebrow. Still, Dimity had said he was coming and despite differences in coloration, he resembled his sister enough for recognition and was almost as pretty. He was something important down at Oxford and had been responsible for bringing along the professor and his common sense. Cris understood that Pillover himself was also going to perform a reading of Catullus. Cris hoped it was one of the less scandalous poems. But since Pillover looked to be a dour, retiring fellow, Cris figured it would be something banal.

He decided he would leave the matter of his own interest in Dimity and any formal introduction as a prospective husband for another time.

However, Professor Pillover Plumleigh-Teignmott had more mettle than expected. For Dimity's brother tracked Cris down, a little later, when Cris was stretching alone in the drawing room before the ravenous brain-hordes arrived.

"See here, you're actually Sir Crispin, are you not?"

"Hush up. I'm Mr Carefull at the moment. We're still keeping up appearances. Otherwise, why would I be practicing for a bloody ballet?"

"Fair jigs. It's only that my sister talks about you all the time. I mean to say, *all the time*." The young man slouched into a small chair as if exhausted by Dimity's enthusiasm.

"That's nice to know."

"Is it? Nice for you, maybe. Put yourself in my position. *All the time*, sir, all the time!"

"Yes, it must be very trying. Now, may I help you with something, or will you leave me to do my *développés* in peace?"

Pillover stood and mooched about for a bit, picking up knick-knacks and putting them down again. Cris resumed warming up.

"You're very muscled, aren't you?" the professor said eventually.

"I try." Cris did not stop what he was doing.

"You're successful, no *trying* needed. She's very fond of your muscles, my sister is. As I have learned, at length." He mooched some more.

Cris kept up his steps, shifting from slower, measured movements to something a little faster, getting the blood pulsing.

"I say, would you pause for just a moment? That's awfully distracting."

Cris stopped and stood, staring down at the man, hands on hips. "So you've figured it out, have you?"

"What?" Pillover looked genuinely confused.

"Whatever it is you need to say to me?" Cris rose on the balls of his feet, then down again.

"Would you please be still?"

Cris sighed and relaxed, forcing himself into perfect posture and activated stillness, as if he were holding a pose.

"It's only..." Pillover got a particular glint in his eye. It was disconcertingly similar to his sister's take-no-prisoners glint. "Look here, don't break her heart, all right? I know your kind from school – nothing but cricket and hunting and such. No finer feelings at all."

"I was rather afraid she might break mine."

"Good. Much better that way."

Cris laughed. "She wants to marry me."

Pillover looked glum. "I know. I heard about it, at *length*, remember?"

"And I want to marry her."

"You don't say? Bally odd, that. Still, I suppose that's all right then. Peculiar of you, of course. I mean to say, she's my sister and she's absolutely ghastly. All that chattering, and the fluffy-fluffy hair, and the bright clothing, and that garish jewelry *all the time*, and then more chatter. And bustling about and always trying to tidy a chap and – oh dear God! – please don't let me put you off!"

Cris laughed and clapped the young man on one shoulder. He did it a bit too hard, because of the dig about the cricket. Pillover stumbled slightly and then straightened and shoved his spectacles up his nose.

"A large part of the appeal, I assure you. Especially the hair."

"Oh, go on with you! Really? I suppose it takes all sorts."

"So I have your permission?" He was Dimity's brother, after all.

"Oh, is that the sort of thing you need? For goodness sake, what have I got to do with it? My opinion has never mattered to Dimity before. Please don't let it start now."

"True, but I should still like it."

"I don't know you at all, Sir Crispin, but your

physique is nothing to complain about, and you seem a decent enough chap, for an athletic sportsman type. I'm not sure about your choice of attire."

"Dimity's choice, I assure you."

"Oh, well then, that explains that. Got you dancing to her tune already, has she?"

"Literally." Cris did a small spin for emphasis.

Pillover nodded. "Proceed, then."

"I shall."

Dimity could not have been more in her element. All the guests arrived. Better still, all of them were dressed appropriately. The port had been served. Small cut-glass bowls of ice cream were taken around, because Dimity didn't do anything by halves and a good impression was mandatory.

Lord Maccon was looming in a nook, pretending interest in the history of plumbing as chronicled in six volumes. He sipped a glass of whiskey and spoke to no one. Lord Finbar and Lord Kirby both gave him a wide berth, noses wrinkled in disgust, but otherwise the werewolf was treated with every courtesy. In fact, if anything, he seemed uncomfortable with the banality of it all. Dimity didn't know what he'd expected, but a pleasant assembly in beautiful accommodations clearly wasn't it. She saw him interview a few of the staff, and watch all vampire interactions with evident surprise. They seemed to be making a good impression. She made sure to attend to him regularly herself, as well.

Beyond Lord Maccon, the conversation flowed as freely as the port. Gantry and his parents mingled happily. In his evening attire, Gantry gave a remarkably good impression of a stuffed goose. His father looked exactly as Gantry would in a few years' time, only less outdoorsy. Mrs Ogdon-Loppes seemed recalcitrant at first, but was quickly won over by Budgy Hall, its library, and the comestibles.

Lord Finbar was having a depressingly fantastic time, discussing the various books of poetry on prominent display in the library with an editor from London. Lord Kirby was also doing well, playing the gallant host and ushering the guests to their seats. Trudge was faithfully by his side, greeting all new arrivals with a big, friendly doggie smile. At least someone in the hive knew how to smile.

Eventually, Justice made her grand entrance in a frilly pink gown with maximum ruffles that floated about her as she descended the stairs. Lord Maccon's expression became one of confused awe.

Gantry went to her and swept her up in his manly arms, but their embrace was blessedly chaste and the purple prose kept to a minimum. He escorted her over to meet his parents, who were wearing expressions of mixed confusion, shock, and delight. Pillover looked relaxed and prepared, Professor Fausse-Maigre equally so. They were both comfortable with the academic lecture circuit or she wouldn't have invited them, but it no doubt helped that they were also deep into the whiskey. Cris was skulking behind the curtains, inside the bay window, keeping limber for his part of the evening's entertainment. Occasionally, he would peek out at Dimity, giving her very arch looks.

Then, just as Lord Finbar took the stage to begin introducing the evening's presenters, Rosie sidled up to Dimity, her face a picture of distress and her cap askew.

Dimity quickly ushered her from the library and away from the guests into the sitting room.

"What is it, my dear?"

"It's Betsy, Mrs Carefull. She was meant to be down feeding the baroness over an hour ago. Mr Theris was going to take her, you being so busy with the event and all."

"Oh bother, I forgot!" She hadn't, of course. This was part of the plan.

"Well, they must never have gone, because the baroness is screaming loud enough to wake the dead and I can't find either of them anywhere. It's all coming up from the scullery and into the kitchen. It's scaring the staff, it is."

Dimity hid a smile – excellent. The baroness was likely annoyed that her routine had been disrupted, but also, hopefully, curious as to why. And if Dimity went in, all full of excitement for the party, what woman could resist the temptation to see what she was on about? Especially since it was, technically, the baroness's own party.

Lord Finbar would be starting his oration soon. Dimity had no intention of stopping him now – he'd lose faith in everything, and all her efforts would crumble into ruin. Which sounded like a line from one of his poems, but was perfectly true.

"I shall have to do it myself," she said for Rosie's benefit. "Good thing I'm wearing this particular dress." Dimity was in one of her more mature evening gowns. It was a lovely ruby red, with a low square neckline, and she'd paired it with one of her more powerful ruby necklaces. The really big one, with the washed gold plating. A kind of battle armor.

"Rosie, go up to my room, please, and fetch the teal brocade that's hanging at the back of my wardrobe. It has all the foundation garments with it, including a funny cage thing that looks like it's meant for birds. Bring it all."

"Yes, ma'am." Rosie scuttled off.

Dimity peeked into the library.

"*I stand alone at the edge of the abyss,*" intoned Lord Finbar. Good, he'd started.

She caught Crispin's eye. She nodded at him to let him know she had everything under control. Then, because she'd promised to trust him and was trying to be more honest about life, she pointed at her neck.

He looked confused.

She made two fingers curl at it with one hand and made a stabby-stabby motion with them.

Cris blanched.

"*All is winter in my heart.*" Lord Finbar clasped a fist to the breast of his emerald satin smoking jacket and cast his eyes to the heavens.

Dimity put a quick finger to her lips and shook her head at Crispin.

Then she mouthed, *The show must go on!*

Cris shook his head at her violently. This momentarily distracted from Lord Finbar's performance in front of the curtains.

"The angels are dead," cried Lord Finbar, lifting both hands to the ceiling.

Dimity made shooing motions at Cris, urging him back behind the curtain.

She turned away – no more time. Rosie had returned holding the teal gown and its bustle, which Dimity had had shipped all the way from Paris.

"Let's get to it, shall we?" Dimity led the way to the trap door, where Rosie helped her pile the dress into her own arms and climb down the stairs.

Dimity didn't let the girl come any further. "You go back, Rosie. Distract Mr Theris if you can find him. I have a feeling he might suddenly show up and try to save the day by coming to the baroness's rescue and we can't have that. I'm expecting a claviger from the Sheffield Pack. He's to be directed to Mr Theris and no other. Also, you need to be there for Lord Finbar, so he can see you clapping as he finishes his poem."

"Yes, ma'am. Of course, ma'am." Rosie scampered off.

Dimity trotted as fast as she could (while holding that much dress) down the long limestone tunnel. All the while, she could hear the angry yelling and near hysterically shrill cries of the hive queen echoing against the stone.

"Where is my dear Betsy? After what was done to me! After what I have suffered. Why does she not come to me? Why must they all leave? Why must I always endure such heartache?"

Dimity reached the door and knocked, loudly. She extracted her key, prepared as always for an infiltration.

"Betsy, is that you?"

"No, Baroness, it's me, Mrs Carefull. I believe we ought to introduce ourselves now, don't you?"

Silence.

She fit the key into the lock and turned. The tumblers gave with a thump.

The door creaked open.

Dimity held up the teal dress before her as if it were a shield. "Isn't this absolutely lovely, Baroness Ermondy? All the way from Paris. And look here, a bustle, the very latest thing."

Baroness Octavine Ermondy was a stunning woman, rail thin and quite tall, with high cheekbones, big blue eyes, a thin-lipped mouth over four prominent fangs, and a mass of gorgeous red hair. She looked profoundly aristocratic and pinched by decades of suspicion.

"Well, yes, that is very nice material. But who are you, child?"

"Oh, you know who I am." If vampires did nothing else, they gossiped, even the crazy ones. She had no doubt Mr Theris (in his biased way) and then Betsy had been keeping the queen well informed on the doings above ground.

"Where's Betsy?" There was a slight tremor in the baroness's voice.

"Unavoidably delayed. Won't I do?" Dimity didn't believe any of it. She knew artifice when it was trembling before her. There was absolutely nothing wrong with this woman, reclusive vampire with threatening Gothic overtones or not!

Dimity gestured at her own throat. It was still

adorned with the large necklace, but nicely displayed by her low-cut gown.

"You do have a lovely neck." The queen's eyes were full of avarice all of a sudden, and her voice lost its hesitancy.

Dimity tilted her head to one side and then the other, pretending to look at the limestone ceiling. "And I come bearing bustle..."

"Yes, I read about those – the new decade brings with it new, ground-breaking fashions for the posterior."

"Superior and flattering ones, don't you feel? Especially for one with a willowy, elegant frame, such as yourself." Dimity moved one step into the room.

"Oh, do you think so? After what was done to me..." The tremble was back. Really, she ought to have gone to Finishing School. There were much better ways to curry sympathy.

"What was done to you, Baroness?" Dimity pushed, just a little.

"Well, I shouldn't..."

Dimity waved the dress at her seductively. "I'm sure I should love to hear all about it. And this dress won't fit me, you know?"

"Come in, dear, do, and let me tell you all about it."

Dimity went in, closing the door firmly behind her.

She missed the fact that Cris was already at the end of the tunnel, trying desperately to chase after her.

Lord Kirby followed Cris when he ran from the library. Cris had managed to evade him all the way down and into the limestone tunnel, not because Cris was faster or more nimble than a vampire, but because until he threw back the cellar door and swung himself to drop down (bypassing the steps), the vampire didn't understand where he was going.

Lord Kirby swung after him easily. "No one but a drone and a meal are meant to be down here! My queen left strict orders!" At the bottom of the stairs, he grabbed Crispin as if he were a scamp of a schoolboy, and not a man desperate with worry for his beloved. The strength in him was frightening, Crispin was no sapling, but the pudgy vampire handled him as if he were no more than a toasting fork.

Now Lord Kirby held him hard and tight at the mouth of the tunnel beneath the hive house. Lord Kirby, who wanted to be praetoriani, who intended to always protect his queen. Lord Kirby, who might look like pudding shaped into a man in a robe, but who was still a vampire. And any vampire was stronger and faster than any human, even Sir Crispin.

Justice, having followed them as well, climbed down after and pressed her hands firmly over Sir Crispin's mouth to keep him from calling out. "We aren't supposed to be down here, Kirby! She banished us from following her here, remember? So we would not see her shame."

"Oh, I remember, but this one is obviously worried about something going on. Let us wait a minute or two more." Lord Kirby shook Crispin a little.

"You're in defiance!" Justice gasped, placing her

free hand to her lips in shock.

The two vampires continued to bicker softly.

Cris had never been so frightened in his life. He'd caught Sparkles shutting the door behind her, locking herself in a cave with a crazed vampire queen. Dimity had carried some fluffy garment in with her but no apparent weapons, and she was wearing a red gown with a very low neckline. Anyone who knew her as Crispin did could only surmise that she had intended this all along. Red to hide the blood.

But how would she do it without fainting?

And how could he trust that this lovely young woman who had made beauty out of darkness, who had transformed a whole hive with her artistic skill, would not be too tempting a prospect for a vampire queen? What if the baroness decided to keep her? What if the baroness wanted to drain her? Horrific visions danced through his head.

Cris struggled in vain against the iron hold of Lord Kirby. He bit hard at the hand of Justice. But the two vampires were like steel around and against him. They had not seen her enter the sanctuary, so they did not know Dimity was in with the queen. And he knew that, though they might like Sparkles, if forced to choose between rescuing his lady and defending theirs, they would always do as ordered by their queen. It was the way of a hive. Neglect notwithstanding, hive-bound vampires never disobeyed their maker.

He had forgotten they were monsters.

How could he have forgotten that?

Above and behind them, having assumed the mad

leap of a dancer from behind the curtains merely a mark of a brief intermission between speakers, the guests clapped politely for Lord Finbar and settled back to listen to Pillover recite Catullus. Pillover, who had no idea what his sister was up to.

So the vampires held Cris tight as may be. And tears of frustration leaked down his face while he stared at the locked cave door and, for the first time in his life, was perfectly still.

"So, you see, it's all Countess Nadasdy's fault. That fanged viper! She's so very womanly in shape and form and she guided fashion down in London, and thus *everywhere* else, further and further into those huge crinolines and hoops and wide sleeves and sloped shoulders and they look *awful* on me!" The hive queen's voice was a whine of deeply felt injustice.

Dimity listened, nodding sympathetically, while she helped the baroness out of her dressing robe and into the bustle and underthings. "I can see how they might, but now fashions are shifting at last."

"Are you certain? I don't understand how Nadasdy could lose her grip on popular taste so thoroughly."

"Well," said Dimity, "let me tell you. London is overrun with werewolves these days. You heard about Lord Maccon? That always affects fashion. And those French hives are not to be discounted, simply because they are in hiding. I mean, not when silhouettes are at stake. Honestly, no one likes a crinoline, not really, not as big as they've become. Ridiculous impractical things, they get caught on just about everything, and they take up so much space. A bustle is so much nicer. There, you see?"

She twirled the hive queen about and stood on a step stool to drop the teal skirt over the vampire's head, fluffing it and fastening it to fall properly over the bustle at the back.

"Only see how this complements your figure? Oh, I should so love to be as tall as you. This sort of dress is beyond flattering when you have the height to carry it off. Shall we try the bodice? Now, please go on, tell me of your troubles... what happened next?"

"Well then, my lovely Lord Rashwallop, my oldest and dearest friend, went all funny. And BUR put him down, like an animal! And he only killed, you know, half a dozen or so people. Really, BUR might have been nicer about it. And after that, well, I had this lovely young drone and she left me. Left *me*! For a career as an opera singer. Said Nottingham was too provincial. At that juncture I took to my bed, it was all too much." Her face pinched and her eyes snapped, more in anger than sorrow. As if she were annoyed to have been left.

"Who wouldn't?" murmured Dimity, sympathetically.

"Then one of my dear drones, he asked if he might try for the bite. Then I would not be so lonely, with my dear Lord Rashwallop gone, if I had another hive member. And so I did bite him, and he died in the attempted metamorphosis. I could withstand no more trials. So I retired here, to my cave and my grief. And the other drones all left me too, and only Mr Theris remained. And he wouldn't let me bite him."

Aha, thought Dimity, *so that was his ploy.* Deny the queen until she was desperate for him and him alone, and thus wholly dependent upon him. It wasn't a bad plan, actually, if one wanted control of a hive in such a way. And didn't know the dangers of isolating a queen and driving her to Goth.

Dimity guided the baroness around to stand and admire herself in a mirror. "But the fashion papers I sent you, these gave you hope?"

"Oh yes, and then lovely, lovely Betsy, such a very sweet girl. I've always had a terrible weakness for milkmaids."

"Well upstairs, Betsy has gone missing, dear Baroness, and not willingly. Frankly, you're desperately needed now. Everyone misses you so very much and we need your help to find her. Besides, you should be seen in a dress as fine as this. You look wonderful!"

The baroness admired herself in the massive gilt mirror against the wall. "I do, don't I?"

"And, of course, if you require a bit of a nibble before we go up, to restore yourself, I'm willing to provide. Although, I am bound to warn you, I shall probably faint. I'm not very good with blood."

"Oh, that is a tragedy. You aren't a new drone candidate, then? Because that would never work. If you were lucky enough to survive the bite, what kind of vampire queen would that make you, who faints at blood?"

The queen flashed her double set of fangs at Dimity, displaying the second, maker set, sharp and wicked large.

Dimity shuddered. "Oh no, you are correct in that assumption. I'm not interested at all in being a vampire. Never was. I'm only here to redecorate. I mean, at first I thought I might, and then I saw your lovely house and I thought what it really needed was some color and then maybe you would love it again."

"Capital," said the queen. "It was getting rather run-down. I forgot to care, you see, about appearances. I should like to see what you've done with the place. It was awfully shabby. Betsy has reminded me there is more to live for than simply fashion."

"And your vampires?"

"I have missed them too. My darlings. I'm sure they have been well enough, no?"

"Oh no, Baroness, they could not function at all without your guidance and attention."

"You didn't step in to fill the breach? You seem a flashy, capable girl."

"Only in matters decorative. They pined for you. They never stopped pining."

"Pined, you say? Isn't that sweet? They are dears, of course. I should be up there with them. But I was so lost to my melancholy, you understand? I forgot about such things, lost to the depths of despair for a while. Until Betsy. And this dress."

"Are you feeling better now, Baroness? Shall we go up, then, and find Betsy? Reunite you with your pining vampires?" Dimity thought now might be the perfect time.

"Yes, dear, let's do that."

As it turned out, it was.

Crispin's knees trembled and he nearly collapsed at the remarkable sight of two women emerging from the limestone cave. First came a tall redhead wearing a teal evening gown of extremely flattering and rather modern proportions. Dimity followed directly after her.

Lord Finbar and Justice instantly let go of Cris.

Cris stumbled forwards.

"Bow, you fool!" hissed Lord Kirby.

Cris bowed, eyes still desperately on Dimity, searching for any sign of injury. Sparkles was walking demurely down the tunnel, a little behind and to the side of the other woman, who could only be the hive queen. Dimity's neck was white and smooth and entirely unblemished.

"Oh, my dearest Lord Kirby, how fine you look tonight. And is that my little Justice? In a pretty pink dress? You look divine, darling, absolutely divine. It's so nice to see you both again, it's been too long. Now come into my arms, my hive, my little loves."

Justice and Lord Kirby rushed to the stately woman and she embraced them, petting them and kissing their cheeks.

"And who is this strapping young specimen of humanity?"

"My husband," Cris heard Dimity say quickly, "Mr Carefull."

"Husband, is he?"

"*My* husband, your ladyship. Mine." Dimity sounded very firm on the matter.

The baroness laughed. "Understood, little bird. Now let us find Betsy."

"Betsy is missing?" Cris straightened, weak with relief, almost shaking, he was so happy to see Dimity whole and unsullied.

Dimity paused to stare at him, her face a picture of concern. "I've never seen you so white."

"I thought you were going to feed her. I thought you might *die*!"

"I was intending the first if necessary, but never the second. And if she took too much, I was prepared to defend myself." She obviously wasn't worried about the vampires overhearing her, no doubt assuming they would think her a silly chit to imagine she could defend herself against any vampire, let alone a queen.

The vampires disappeared up the limestone steps, Justice and Lord Kirby solicitous and worshipful of their hive queen's resurrection.

Dimity shifted aside, using Crispin's body to shield her from their view. She reached up to the enormous, ornate ruby necklace she wore about her neck. Cris had grown so accustomed to her ostentatious taste, he'd not even really noticed it.

She pressed the largest jewel and with a quiet snap, a sharp wooden spike ejected from behind the necklace, pointing downwards.

"I had it designed specially," said Dimity, proudly. "When have you ever known me to be unprepared, my dearest tuppenny knight?"

"Are all your sparkles deadly?"

"Every fabulous one of them."

"I love you."

"As you very well should, considering I feel the same. I'm delighted my jewelry has forced a confession at last."

"What else would do it?"

She twinkled at him, hazel eyes squinted in pleasure. "So, husband mine, one last performance before Mr and Mrs Carefull retire for good?"

"And we have to find Betsy," he reminded her.

Betsy, as it turned out, had been locked in the silver cabinet. A room to which, mind you, since the departure of the butler, only Mr Theris had the key. Given the queen's caterwauling, no one had heard her on the other side of the scullery. They let her out, gave her a small fortifying glass of port, and saw her set to rights.

Mr Theris was outside in the back gardens, being seduced by a werewolf claviger from Sheffield who'd come down especially to do nothing more than exactly that. When confronted about his ill conduct, and informed that the queen had emerged, he declared himself thoroughly disappointed in the whole lot of them. And that they could hang for all he cared – he was going to Sheffield. Dimity said she had very little doubt about the hive's eagerness to release him from his drone contract. And she intended to make that a truth as soon as could be.

Dimity and Crispin returned to the house to find the baroness graciously holding court in the library. Lord Maccon still watched with interest from his lurking book nook, only he was now eating ice cream and looking moderately more relaxed. Meanwhile, an adoring crowd of interested intellectuals hung on Baroness Ermondy's every word. They seemed to think she was one of the speakers for the evening.

"How wonderfully existential," Dimity heard one gentleman say to another.

"Oh, Mrs Carefull," the hive queen said, when Dimity walked in, "so very kind of you to arrange this little gathering to welcome me back above ground. And what you've done to Budgy Hall, quite exceptional. I shall recommend your talents in the matter of furnishings and wallpaper to all of my friends."

A round of introductions was required then. Justice had to present Gantry to the queen, while carefully not calling her a queen or a vampire, the implication being that Justice was the baroness's ward and Gantry her prospective suitor. The baroness thought Gantry *nicely robust and meaty* (which the watchers took to mean he would be an excellent father to healthy heirs), and said that *of course* he could come live with them if it made Justice happy (which the watchers thought a little odd, but then the very wealthy were often quite eccentric in matters of marriage). Dimity understood this to mean that he would soon become an official drone, which would make Justice very happy.

The visiting intellectuals sat in enthralled fascination. They murmured questions to one another, discussing the allegorical nature of this particular piece. Were the performative introductions meant to symbolize man's frail relationship to his own conception of social constructs within the context of a broader society?

Then the queen commented that Lord Finbar looked very handsome in green, and wasn't Rosie a lovely little creature, and of course she could be official too. After all, she herself intended Betsy for permanence, and the more the merrier.

Dimity knew both young ladies were soon to be drones as well, but one audience member explained to his friend that he thought it "a commentary on the transformative nature of the aristocracy."

"Yes, yes, but would you look at her dress! It's too modern for the aristocracy. Surely it's a statement on the conflicts inherent in a class-driven system?" objected his companion.

Then the hive's new Corgi had to be introduced as well. He looked up at his new mistress all big eyes and huge ears, madly wagging a tail he didn't have. Baroness Ermondy was charmed into complete submission.

She stood and produced from some secret stash about her person a collection of blank Valentine's cards. These she cast out in a wild flutter into the crowd. "I shall not need them anymore," she proclaimed.

The charmed crowd applauded politely.

"Very existential," reiterated the gentleman to his friend.

"Yes, but what does it *mean*?" lamented the other.

"Meaning is not important. That is the entire *point* – the *search* for meaning is what matters, you see? What are we but questions? Who are we really, what is there but the search itself? Hence, the casting of the blank cards."

"I didn't get that at all. Really, Arlington, why must you insist on attending these bloody things?"

"Hush now, there's one more coming. And I insist on attending because everyone should broaden his mind, Quattermud, even you. Do try to keep up."

The baroness ceded the limelight, taking a seat in the front row next to Lord Finbar. She expressed regret at having missed the first two orations, and thanked him for his thoughtfulness in reserving her a seat.

Dimity grinned. What more did a vampire want in afterlife, after emerging from six months of seclusion in a cave, than a presentation on the higher nature of common sense while a man interpreted it balletically? That was, after all, what was up next.

The crowd quieted once more, most of them apparently under the impression that they had just witnessed an allegory so brilliant, it eluded even their intellects. Dimity had no doubt that more than one paper would be written on this evening's events in the months to come.

Lord Kirby sat on the other side of Baroness Ermondy. She had not yet been told of his wish to increase rank in the hive, and of Lord Finbar's to be reduced, but Dimity had no doubt of their success. The dog lay at their feet. Rosie sat beside Lord Finbar while on Lord Kirby's other side, Justice cuddled next to Gantry, Betsy at the end of the row. Mr Theris was (presumably) still in the garden being seduced to the furry side.

Dimity was very, very pleased with herself. She sat

near the back, where she could keep an eye on *everything*.

The final performance of the evening began.

Professor Fausse-Maigre droned on in typical academic style as to the nature of truth and the importance of scientific inquiry. He talked about reason and ethical grounding and the profundity of logic. But meanwhile, ah, *meanwhile*, Sir Crispin, behind him, pranced about performing an impressive arabesque every time the word *higher* was used, small leaps at the word *truth*, and those double knee-bend things whenever the man spoke of *logic* or *reason*.

It was certainly something to behold.

Something.

Dimity enjoyed the play of muscles on Sir Crispin's arms and back, the line of his long legs, and the way he pointed his toes just so.

And when Professor Fausse-Maigre ended with a flourish and a bow, Crispin whipped into a perfect pirouette. The assembled company surged to their feet and erupted into resounding applause.

Certainly, they had just witnessed greatness.

Certainly, they had witnessed *remarkably innovative and deeply moving* originality.

Certainly, they would never again witness anything like it in their lifetimes.

Especially if Sir Crispin had anything to say about it.

Dimity turned up the gas, brightening the room, and bustled out to the kitchen encouraging the newly hired staff to serve the whiskey now, and some sugared fruit.

The rest of the night was a veritable triumph.

The hive queen mingled with her new friends, her gown received endless compliments, the death of the crinoline heralded by most ladies present with profound relief.

"Just think, it will make these gatherings much easier to manage. Not to be crashing and bashing about so! I have nearly upended three tables and a chair already," lamented one elderly matron.

Dimity glided amongst the intellectuals. Her brother was trapped in a corner, surrounded by several young ladies of marriageable age, which always happened to him at parties. Poor old sod. He was telling them, in excruciating detail, about his current research into the grammatical construction of Roman political speeches.

Professor Fausse-Maigre, who proved to be rather shy and retiring when he was not speaking on matters well rehearsed, had found his way to the piano in the drawing room and was plonking at it with some skill. The ladies in the corner eventually dragged Pillover, Justice, Gantry, and a few others off to that room to dance.

Mrs Ogdon-Loppes summoned Dimity over with an autocratic finger. She and her husband, having consumed six glasses of whiskey between them, were sitting rather floppily together on one of more plush leather sofas.

"Mrshh Carefull. You lovely thing, you! Gantry tells us thissh is all your fault."

Dimity went over to them with alacrity. "Oh, I assure you it is not so, madam. I am a mere instrument of aesthetic order."

"Well, whatever you did, it fixed my son's instrument right up, now, didn't it," blustered Mr Ogdon-Loppes, a little too loudly.

Mrs Ogdon-Loppes guffawed. "Oh, Henry, you're too droll!" She tried to lower her voice to a whisper, but it more closely resembled a hissing roar. Dimity didn't mind.

"We thought he'd formed an inappropriate connection to a young local lad – you know how it goesh, dear. A right ruffian, we thought. They kept meeting in woods, if you would believe it. Woods! So muddy. Gantry always did have an obsession with Robin Hood. We suspected something quite low indeed, a highwayman, or perhashpss even flywaymen." Mrs Ogdon-Loppes nodded so hard she drifted forwards and began to slide off the couch.

Dimity steadied her, smiling at them both.

Mr Ogdon-Loppes picked up the story. "And here we find instead such a lovely, respectable young thing, all proper, and a *girl* besides! Never expected a girl. Not of Gantry. Blasted brilliant, that is!"

Mrs Ogdon-Loppes recovered her tongue, if not her head, which kept nodding, only now from side to side. "It's really quite extraordsh... Extraordinarish... great! And we understand the family is well connected. Titled. Little Justice isn't, erm, the heir, is she?"

"I'm afraid not. But she is very well set up. Your Gantry will never want for anything."

"Oh, of courshh, of courshh not." Mrs Ogdon-Loppes went serious, still nodding.

Mr Ogdon-Loppes started nodding along with his

wife. "Too much to ask, that. Still, it seems like an excellent match for a third son. It's enough to know the family likes our Gantry. We never expected him to amount to much, quite honestly. All that larking about on horseback and riding after foxes."

"You're pleased, then, with the match?" Dimity was having rather too much fun with the nodding Ogdon-Loppeses. Someday soon they'd likely need to be told their son was taking drone status with a vampire hive, not actually marrying into a family of extremely esoteric aristocrats. But that would require a more private audience with the baroness. Dimity had no doubt that a satisfactory blood dowry could be arrived at, and the couple seemed progressive enough to accept this alternate outcome with grace and discretion. At least, Dimity hoped so.

"Profundently. Couldn't have worked out better, really."

Dimity arched her brows. "I couldn't agree more."

Cris was next to her then, having gone and changed and come back down looking perfectly respectable and completely handsome in a pristine evening suit.

Together they approached Lord Maccon, who, having apparently finished all of the ice cream and most of the whiskey, was looking twitchy and eager to leave.

"You two, pirouettes indeed," he growled at them, not really angry. He seemed to be rather a growly person. Dimity knew the type – her friend Sidheag was very like him. Not unsurprising, actually, since the two were distantly related.

"Is everything all right, sir?" asked Dimity.

"Could use something raw to eat," grumbled the werewolf.

"No, sir, is *everything* all right?" She pressed the advantage afforded her by the success of the evening.

He coughed. "Aye. Aye. Bloody waste of my time, coming here. Place seems bally well in order. Not sure what the fuss was about. Bah. I'm off. Might I make use of your cloakroom for the night? I hear there's good rabbit hunting 'round these parts."

Dimity took that to mean he wished to strip, change shape, hunt, and then return later.

"I'm sure that would be fine, Lord Maccon," she said, feeling very gracious in her victory.

He nodded at them both. "I bid you good evening. Sir. Madam."

They waved the werewolf off.

"All done, then, Sparkles?"

"Yes, my tuppenny knight, I made it all quite pretty in the end. Look at how happy they all are. And it's lovely and tidy."

"Very good, my love."

"And you even ended on a pirouette."

"Only the very best for my Sparkles."

EPILOGUE

Dimity married her tuppenny knight in modest style, although her dress was so very fashionable there were some who claimed that she singlehandedly started the new trend for very impressive bustles. However, she was careful to credit the Nottingham Hive queen when anyone asked her directly. She wore dangling opal earrings, and an opal poison ring (just in case) to match her new wedding ring (more opals), because her husband paid attention and was an extremely thoughtful man. Fortunately, the ceremony went off without a hitch, and there was no reason for her to test the usefulness of any of her jewelry – least of all the wedding ring.

To everyone's delight, Sir Crispin's wastrel of a father was found to have not, in fact, squandered the entire family fortune, but instead invested it in a rather impressive jewelry collection discovered in a butter churn, which he left to his only son. But despite her vast options, the new Lady Bontwee was noted to have a marked preference for those opal earrings.

Upon returning from an extended tour of the

Mediterranean, Lady Bontwee spent her days happily guiding her adored husband into becoming a prominent member of Parliament. She threw numerous, increasingly desirable evening parties to which she wore her inherited jewelry (only lightly *modernized* to her exacting standards of deadliness) and which resulted in rather unprecedented political influence. Possibly because of Dimity, possibly because of the jewelry.

She mostly behaved like a lady, and to all appearances had given up her Honey Bee ways and War Office position, becoming nothing more than a *grande dame* of London society. Whether this was the truth or not, who's to tell? The government certainly had no record of anything subversive.

Sir Crispin and Lady Bontwee produced, in embarrassingly rapid succession, five boy children, who entirely cured their mother of any inclination to faint at the sight of blood.

The family visited their friends at Budgy Hall regularly, and always knew all the gossip. Eventually Dimity and her tuppenny knight took a country seat outside of Nottingham – a smallish Grecian-inspired mansion on a stream – called Coot's Crest. It boasted a diminutive thatched-roof cottage in the back named Coot's Bottom. The couple kept some very discreet servants who never mentioned to anyone that a tough-looking lady with sharp green eyes and a dark-skinned man with nighttime habits (Dimity's true friends, as she always called them), stayed at Coot's Bottom regularly. And if, upon occasion, Lady Bontwee and her husband were seen skittering down the garden path in trailing dressing gowns, and laughing uproariously into the wee hours of the night, well, every toff has a few eccentricities.

As Justice would have it, we should all be so lucky as to go wafting about dramatically in a trailing nightgown on occasion.

AUTHOR'S NOTE

Thank you so much for reading *Defy or Defend*. If you enjoyed it, or if you would like to read more about any of my characters, please say so in a review. I'm grateful for the time you take to do so.

I have a silly gossipy newsletter called the Chirrup. I promise: no spam, no fowl. (Well, maybe a little fowl and the occasional giveaway.)

gailcarriger.com

AUTHOR AFTERTHOUGHTS

Before you ask, *Defy or Defend* is indeed an ode to the fantastic *Cold Comfort Farm* by Stella Gibbons. Try the charming book or the adorable movie. You won't be sorry. I always knew *Cold Comfort Farm* was a reverse Gothic, but it wasn't until I started researching for this book that I realized it was also a makeover story.

I do love a makeover and so, it turns out, does Dimity.

Dimity is an ode to my (as Dimity would put it) true friend Phrannish. Whom we all knew would end up in a Gothic novel with a tuppenny knight at some point. Sorry it took me so long. Not sorry I turned velvet into the bad guy (insert evil laugh here).

The Corgi puppy is based off my first Corgi friend, Mr Chumley Zimmerman, combined with the charming Corbin Drake. Find more about Corbin via my lovely author friend, Piper J Drake.

Budgy Hall is based on the Lace Market Hotel in downtown Nottingham. Yes, it does in fact overlook an old graveyard, but I promise, it's not gloomy at all, and is a lovely place to stay. Nottingham is, in fact, riddled with limestone caves. It's always been strange to me that none of the many Robin Hood retellings mention them. When I lived there, I worked inside one. And that's all you get to hear about that. A girl's gotta have some secrets.

The epilogue in this story was originally written for *Manners & Mutiny*, the final Finishing School book. I pulled it from M&M because I wanted to write the Delightfully Deadly series. And... here we are.

Did all the Finishing School young ladies get epilogues?

Why, yes. Yes, they did.

Thank you for reading, my dear ones. May we all find our safety and our sparkles, in whatever form they take.